OVER THE HILL

BY CRAIG DILOUIE

Crash Dive, Episode #1: Crash Dive

Crash Dive, Episode #2: Silent Running

Crash Dive, Episode #3: Battle Stations

Crash Dive, Episode #4: Contact!

Crash Dive, Episode #5: Hara-Kiri

Crash Dive, Episode #6: Over the Hill

One of Us

Suffer the Children

The Retreat, Episode #1: Pandemic

The Retreat, Episode #4: Alamo

The Alchemists

The Infection

The Killing Floor

Children of God

Tooth and Nail

The Great Planet Robbery

Paranoia

OVER THE HILL

A NOVEL OF THE PACIFIC WAR

CRAIG DILOUIE

OVER THE HILL
A novel of the Pacific War
©2018 Craig DiLouie. All rights reserved.

President Harry Truman's speech after the Hiroshima bombing, and Admiral Charles Lockwood's communication to the
Submarine Force after the Japanese surrender, are excerpts
of their actual communications.

Editing by Timothy Johnson.
Cover art by Eloise Knapp Design.
Book layout by Ella Beaumont.

Published by ZING Communications, Inc.

www.CraigDiLouie.com

Most Holy Spirit! Who didst brood
Upon the chaos dark and rude,
And bid its angry tumult cease,
And give, for wild confusion, peace;
Oh, hear us when we cry to Thee,
For those in peril on the sea!

—*From the United States Navy Hymn*

Homo homini lupus

—*Roman adage meaning, "Man is a wolf to man."*

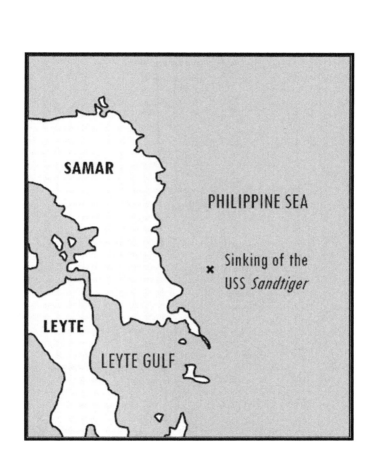

SAMAR

PHILIPPINE SEA

× Sinking of the
USS *Sandtiger*

LEYTE

LEYTE GULF

CHAPTER ONE

THE FURY

Captain Charlie Harrison watched the Philippine Sea swallow the *Sandtiger's* bow. Floating on the surface, his body bobbed on the swells, though his spirit went down with his ship.

A faulty torpedo had sunk his boat.

As the bow disappeared, he hoped the suction of his sinking command might drag him to the bottom with her. There was only a gentle tug, like a farewell, followed by a swirl of bubbles boiling to the surface and a blooming oil slick.

Suspended in the current, Charlie had become a fly on a vast tapestry of violence still playing out all around him. The steel leviathans of great warships filled his view, blasting their giant guns. Tremendous splashes soared past their gunwales. Planes roared through the smoky sky, dodging tracers and shedding bombs that fireballed across decks.

The destroyer that had been intent on ramming

the *Sandtiger* raced toward him. In the distance, a heavy cruiser, flying the Rising Sun, exhaled an angry burst of steam as it sank into the foam. Beyond, the *Yamato* lurched on, blasting its whistle as it continued to veer out of formation.

Hit twice by torpedoes, the battleship had a slight list but was still afloat. Charlie had failed to sink the giant, though he'd put it out of action for now.

He wheeled in the water toward his own side of the conflict and saw the USS *Johnston* dying.

Hardly recognizable as a warship now, the destroyer was a burning husk racked by internal explosions. Japanese destroyers paced in a semi-circle around it, enfilading it with their five-inch guns.

The DD rolled until it capsized and began to sink. An enemy destroyer moved in to deliver the *coup de grace*.

After a heroic stand, the American destroyers had been wiped out, and despite the *Sandtiger*'s Hail Mary attack against the Japanese flagship, there was nothing to stop the juggernaut now.

He spun again, treading water, as the enemy destroyer loomed overhead, its gray steel V stirring up a pronounced bow wake. From the forecastle, Japanese sailors wearing dark blue winter uniforms gazed at him.

One by one, they raised bolt-action rifles and aimed.

It's okay, he told himself.

He didn't sink his boat. He didn't kill most of his sixty-man crew. A jammed rudder on a faulty torpedo did.

It didn't change the fact he was the one who'd pulled the trigger.

Go ahead. Do it.

Spike, Braddock, and rest of the *Sandtiger*'s able crew were now either dead or trapped in a metal coffin bound for the bottom of the Philippine Sea. Rusty, Morrison, and the rest of the men who'd escaped were missing, out of sight.

Take your best shot.

Charlie wasn't sure what came after this, but it offered a sure release from hell.

They didn't shoot. The destroyer lowered a whaleboat from the side.

He ignored it, entranced by the sky. A drifting pall of black smoke dimmed the rising sun to a hazy disc.

Then hands grabbed him and hauled him from the sea. Dumped him like a wet rag on the boat's deck.

Japanese sailors stared down at him with contempt.

He was now a prisoner of the empire.

CHAPTER TWO

NAME, RANK, AND SHIP

The sailors dragged Charlie to the whaleboat's stern and tossed him next to Rusty, Percy, and Morrison, who sat slumped with rope tightly binding their wrists. This done, they began to row back toward their destroyer while one stood over the defeated Americans, gripping his rifle with bayonet affixed.

"Glad to see you living, brother," Rusty muttered.

"You too," Charlie said, words failing to express how relieved he felt to find his friend alive. "Is this it?"

"The Japs didn't care about the other guys who made it off. They only wanted the officers, anybody wearing khaki."

"If I'd known what they were up to, I would have taken my shirt off and taken my chances in the water," Morrison said.

The question was why. Why did the destroyer

stop in a raging battle to pick them up? What was so important about them? It made no sense.

Percy looked at him with a dazed and miserable expression. "Nix?"

Charlie shook his head, and the communications officer lowered his head to his knees. "Sorry, Percy. He was a good man."

The *Akizuki*-class destroyer loomed over them. The gig thudded against the hull under the giant meatball, the Rising Sun insignia of the Imperial fleets. Sailors connected the guy lines and grabbed the monkey ropes for the bumpy ride. The anchor windlass heaved the boat up to the boom.

The Japanese rigged the accommodation ladder over the side, allowing the Americans to cross over to the destroyer's deck. Around them, the *Akizuki*'s crew manned guns, put out fires, ran messages, conducted damage control.

A gaunt officer barked an exchange with their guard, who stood at ramrod attention. Then the officer smiled at his prisoners, projecting a sudden oasis of calm in the middle of the chaotic battle. "Name, rank, and ship, please."

Morrison glanced at Charlie, who nodded slightly while still looking straight ahead. A Hellcat howled through the air and strafed the stern with its six Browning machine guns. The rounds rattled and pinged off the superstructure.

By the time the Americans ducked, the plane had already zipped out of sight.

The officer didn't even flinch. "Name, rank, and ship, please."

"Lieutenant Lester Franklin Morrison, the USS *Sandtiger*."

Rusty and Percy went next. Then it was Charlie's turn. The massive guns of a battleship crashed in a full salvo, the sound thudding through his chest.

"Lieutenant Harry Johnston," he said. "Engineering officer, the *Sandtiger*."

Charlie wore the service khakis of an officer, but otherwise, no insignia denoted his rank. He'd been told the Japanese tortured submarine captains to gain useful intelligence. Maybe it was propaganda, maybe not. He wasn't taking any chances. If he hid his rank, he could protect his secrets.

As far as the Japanese were concerned, Captain Harrison went down with his ship, which, when he thought about it, was only partly a lie.

Another carrier plane howled overhead, chased by the sparks of AA rounds. Its shadow flickered over the boat.

"Our captain is interested in meeting you," the officer said.

As the sailors shoved Charlie across the deck,

he wondered what that might mean, whether good or bad.

Likely, very bad.

CHAPTER THREE

DUTY'S PRICE

The Japanese took the Americans below decks to a storage room barely larger than the average bathroom back at the Royal Hawaiian. They untied the ropes chafing the men's wrists, shoved them inside, and secured the heavy door.

Exhausted, the submariners slumped on the hot, stifling compartment's deck and listened to the muffled roar of outgoing AA fire.

Before going below decks, Charlie had spotted the Japanese warships' curved wakes. They'd halted their advance and were turning to port. The big guns had fallen silent. Maybe Third Fleet was coming. With Third Fleet behind and Seventh Fleet ahead, the Americans would smash the Japanese like a nutcracker.

Charlie doubted he'd survive a second sinking today, but he had a more immediate concern for himself and his men.

"The captain wants to meet us," he said. "That means he wants information."

"Maybe he wants to know how we sank ourselves," Percy said. "How the goddamn Navy destroyed one of their own boats with their shitty fish."

Back in 1911, the Navy had installed a part in each torpedo that neutered the exploder if the fish deviated more than 110 degrees from its original course. For reasons Charlie couldn't fathom, it stopped building them into new torpedoes.

Torpedoes didn't fire straight out of the tube. They often needed to turn during the run to the target. In combat, the TDC automatically transmitted a firing angle to torpedo gyroscopes, devices that measured and maintained angles. When leaving the tube, the torpedo rudder shifted to the side of the desired turn and straightened out as the gyro regulated.

Sometimes, the gyro failed or a sailor failed to set it properly, while other times the rudder jammed. Rarely, but it happened. Charlie had heard horror stories of submarines barely dodging their own fish.

The *Sandtiger* hadn't been so lucky.

"Maybe," Percy added, "the captain just wants to thank us for doing his work for him."

"My guess is the countermeasures," Rusty said.

"The Jap skipper must have seen us firing them from amidships."

Charlie nodded. "He wants to know if we have a new weapon."

"What's our story?" Percy asked.

"That it's ridiculous. Boats don't shoot from the sides. Their eyes were playing tricks on them."

"We're not supposed to say anything at all," Morrison said. "And they're not allowed to make us."

The 1929 Geneva Convention forbade coercing prisoners into giving any information other than name, rank, and serial number. The Japanese hadn't signed the treaty, though in 1942 they had agreed to abide by its terms.

They also ignored them.

"We need to be prepared for the possibility they *will* make us," Charlie said. "What to say and what not to in case they decide on harsh methods."

He didn't have to spell out what those methods meant. *Torture.*

"So what are the rules?" Rusty said.

"If they ask anything about the boat, answer to your best ability. Give them more than they ask."

Morrison's face reddened. "That's treason!"

"The *Sandtiger* was a *Gato* class. Trust me, they've got a copy of *Jane's Fighting Ships*. Probably our manuals too. They already know all about it. If the Japs catch you lying, they'll make you wish you hadn't. The more honest you are, the more you can lie about things that matter. Like the latest retrofits, the countermeasures. They ask about that or anything else, just say it's above your pay grade."

"Our duty isn't over just because we got captured, sir."

"For Chrissakes," Percy said, "listen to the captain."

"Captain Harrison went down with his ship," Charlie reminded them. He locked eyes with Morrison. "Consider what I said his last order and his responsibility."

The torpedo officer turned away. "Aye, aye."

"We're going to do our duty. We're also going to survive."

Rusty eyed Charlie with concern, as if wondering how much of him actually did go down with the *Sandtiger*. "You know, the captain would be proud. We hit that bastard. The *Yamato*. I'm sure of it."

Charlie leaned back against the hot bulkhead, which vibrated from another burst of AA fire. "Twice."

Morrison's sour expression broke into a grin. It was exactly what he'd expect from *Hara-kiri*. The man had taken part in an event that one day might be legend, if anybody survived to tell the tale.

"We really hit him?" Morrison asked.

"The captain did good," Rusty said. "He did his duty."

The torpedo officer was still beaming. "Then what we did…"

Charlie closed his eyes. "We barely hurt him."

"I was going to say what we did was worth it."

Maybe he was right. The Japanese fleet had stopped advancing soon after the *Sandtiger*'s fish had detonated against the *Yamato*'s hull. Maybe in some way the torpedoes had changed the battle's outcome. Often, only results proved the difference between brave and foolhardy.

Charlie pictured the *Sandtiger* tumbling into the Philippine Trench, some of the deepest waters in the Pacific. Long before she touched the seafloor, the colossal pressures would crush her steel hull like an egg.

No, he decided. Whatever the outcome, it hadn't been worth it.

CHAPTER FOUR

THE SKIPPER

The door opened. A blue-uniformed sailor entered, set a tray on the deck in front of them as if it were a last supper, and left.

The meager rations consisted of hardtack, water, and a little rice.

After the meal, the hours rolled by. The room grew hotter and even more stifling. Sweat came in waves, and thirst mounted. They banged on the door for water and a trip to the head. The guard yelled at them in Japanese and did nothing. Angry, they relieved themselves in a bucket.

Charlie sensed the ship turning again. This time, its course held steady. The Japanese were retreating. They'd had Leyte in the bag but had milled around for two hours regrouping before steaming north. American planes had strafed and bombed them all afternoon until their attacks tapered off.

At any moment, he expected to hear Third

Fleet's guns, but Halsey didn't show. The Japanese admiral had simply quit. It was a day of wonders.

The men dozed. Charlie couldn't sleep. When he closed his eyes, he saw the torpedo arcing toward his boat, the awful flash. He had a feeling he'd see that flash again, over and over, the rest of his life.

Men marched and stopped outside the door, which opened to reveal a petty officer and squad of sailors armed with rifles. Their faces smug or scornful, the sailors stared at him. The officer wrinkled his nose at the smell, and his black eyes narrowed. He barked at the Americans in his foreign tongue and beckoned.

"This doesn't look good," Percy said.

"Remember what I said," Charlie told them.

The submariners hauled themselves to their feet and submitted to rebinding of their wrists. Percy was right. This didn't look good. Shambling after the petty officer, they navigated passageways and a ladder that led to the pilothouse, which was located under the captain's bridge.

Charlie took it all in at a glance. The officers in their neat and spotless dark blue winter uniforms. The helmsman behind the ship's wheel and rudder indicator. The gyroscope providing true heading beside its backup magnetic compass. A radar station alive with the sweep of a green light wave.

16

Outside, it was night. Through the windows, he saw vast shadows moving in formation, trailed by phosphorescent wakes. The night was calm with large swells coming astern. Difficult for steering, but the ships moved in perfect lines.

Say what you wanted about the Japanese, they knew how to run a navy.

His eyes settled on a taciturn officer with a peaked cap fitted on his bald skull. A distinct military bearing and natural authority made him stand out from the others. With an unreadable expression and his mouth set in a downward slash, he evaluated his ragged prisoners.

The captain.

The officer who'd welcomed them aboard said, "I am Lieutenant Saito. This is Captain Kondo of the *Akasuki*. He wanted to meet your commander."

Ropes biting their wrists, the Americans shifted their feet, unsure what this meant.

Charlie cleared his throat and said, "Captain Harrison died with his ship."

"As I informed my captain. Captain Harrison's loss is understandable, if regrettable."

Saito talked to Captain Kondo, who responded with quiet authority. Charlie steeled himself for questioning. How they answered would decide the captain's next move. Would determine whether they were tortured for the information.

They just had to be believable. Charlie prayed Morrison went along and didn't play the tough guy. If he did, the captain would conclude they were hiding something, and he'd stop at nothing to get it.

Charlie didn't know how he'd stand up to abuse. He'd volunteered for this war to be tested, and the war had shown him, often severely, what he was made of. The man he'd become under the horrors of torture, however, was not a man he wished to meet.

Saito translated, "Captain Kondo wanted to tell you in person that you and your commander fought bravely and that it was an honor to meet you in combat."

To Charlie's astonishment, the captain saluted the survivors of the *Sandtiger*.

CHAPTER FIVE

DINING WITH THE ENEMY

In the wardroom, the Japanese officers knelt on cushions set around a low table. Freshly washed and wearing dry clothes, Charlie and his men did likewise as instructed. The Japanese skipper sat at the head of the table. In front of the door, two guards stood at the order arms rifle position, bayonets affixed.

Stewards brought hot steamed towels to wipe their hands followed by bowls of clear soup and rice topped with raw fish. The Americans tensed at every movement, but the battle was long over; there was nothing to fight. They blinked at each other in a daze, completely lost, still absorbing this surreal experience.

The Japanese officers produced ornate wooden boxes and removed their personal chopsticks, resting them on small stands. The stewards laid out silverware for the Americans.

The skipper remained silent throughout this

strangely formal preparation. *"Itadakimasu,"* he grunted, and the officers started eating and pouring each other little cups of warm rice wine Saito called *"sake."* Charlie had heard of it but had never tried it.

Percy tested his with a sip, sighed happily, and downed it like a shot.

The captain raised his cup, his officers mirroring the action. Head bowed, the commander gravely spoke in staccato Japanese until Charlie caught the word, *"Sandtiger."*

Across the table, Americans and Japanese drank in respectful silence.

The skipper hadn't captured them. He'd *rescued* them from the sea. Out of respect.

Saito raised his cup. *"Kanpai!"*

"Kanpai!" the officers said and drank again.

One of them smirked at Charlie and yelled, *"Banzai!"*

The submariners jumped, which made the Japanese laugh. *"Banzai!"* they shouted and drank, hurrying to refill each other's cups.

Morrison bristled, but Charlie cautioned him with a glance. The Japanese watched as he raised his cup and drained it, prompting another round of laughter.

The Japanese thought Charlie didn't know what the word meant and had tricked him into toasting long life for the emperor. Charlie played along because, as long as they were feeding his men and otherwise not harming them, he didn't care. After enduring years of hazing as a junior officer in the U.S. Navy, this was nothing.

Satisfied they'd taught the *gaijin* a lesson, the officers went back to slurping their soup. Charlie declined more *sake*, which was already making him feel woozy, and dug into his supper, suddenly ravenous.

At the end of the tasty meal, Saito straightened his dishes and lit a cigarette. He offered one to Charlie. "I hope you will answer a question."

Charlie hadn't smoked since Saipan. He took a drag and reeled at the head rush, taking a moment to prepare for whatever Saito might ask. "What's that?"

"Which of our destroyers holed you?" He added slyly, "Was it the *Akasuki*?"

Charlie passed the smoke to a grateful Percy. "Probably. It was hard to tell."

No need to tell him about the faulty torpedo. That the American Navy had torpedo problems was probably common knowledge in its Japanese counterpart. Still, it was best to say as little as possible as long as he had a choice.

"We wondered if one of your torpedoes had malfunctioned. Your torpedoes are not very good."

Morrison muttered, "We did okay with them anyway, don't you think?"

Charlie held his poker face. "Yours are very good. The best in the world, in fact. I've always envied that about you." It was the simple truth, not flattery.

Saito puffed out his chest. "Yes, they are. The best."

"Maybe you could answer a question, if you don't mind me asking."

"You may ask."

"Why did you retreat?" Charlie said. "Off Samar?"

The lieutenant shrugged. "I am not certain myself."

"You had us on the ropes."

"The 'ropes'?"

"I meant to say you were on the verge of a great victory."

"Admiral Kurita obviously thought otherwise. The battle was chaotic. Our forces had spread out so far they were over the horizon. And your torpedoes forced his ship off the line. He took on water and had to reduce his speed."

The *Sandtiger*'s attack had disrupted the Japanese formation. She'd damaged the *Yamato* and forced him to withdraw from his fleet. As a result, the Japanese admiral had lost tactical awareness and control.

Charlie still didn't think it was worth the price, but it was possible the *Sandtiger*'s sacrifice had accomplished something good.

The Japanese officer hoisted a bottle of *sake* and refilled Charlie's cup. "I hope we can speak more. I haven't talked to an American in years, and it is interesting to hear your perspective on the war. It has been a long, glorious, and bloody road."

Charlie returned the favor by refilling Saito's cup. "It has," he agreed, though right now he saw little glory in it.

"And now, let us drink once more." The officer proposed a toast. "To the day this war is over and we can be friends again instead of enemies."

CHAPTER SIX

KURE

The Americans stewed in the tiny storage compartment with nothing to do but ponder their bleak future. With each passing hour, the shock of the *Sandtiger*'s sinking wore off, and their isolation and loss of liberty set in.

The Japanese treated them to a courteous minimum of comfort. Bedding at night, regular hot meals, and a bucket of soapy water each morning. When the *Akasuki* docked at Formosa for provisioning, the Japanese allowed them to stretch their legs on the deck.

Their captors weren't living up to their brutal reputation, and with no control over his own fate, nothing to fight, Charlie had no focus for his boiling anger except the Bureau of Ordnance and its inability to produce good torpedoes.

Restless and irritable, the men sweated. Morrison whiled away the time plotting escape. Charlie stopped shutting down his hopes and let him ramble. The man obviously needed it.

At last, Rusty cut him off. "Still think you're in a movie, Morrison?"

"They grabbed me out of the water. I never surrendered."

He sounded like Tanaka, who'd told Charlie almost the exact same thing in the Japan Sea.

"Either way, we're prisoners now," Charlie said. "The war's over for us."

The sooner Morrison stopped trying to control his fate, the sooner he could adjust to this new reality. Otherwise, it would eat him up.

Never had Charlie seen greater wisdom in Percy's advice to let things go. The communications officer seemed to be getting along fine. He was alive, right now, and that was enough for him. Mostly, he just seemed bored. If the Japanese asked him to swab their decks, he probably would have happily complied.

Charlie added, "If we're in a movie, it's a Jap movie now. Their story."

He didn't judge Morrison. It was eating him up too. A part of him hoped as much as the young officer did for some way out. Charlie still believed *his* life was a movie, and he was the star. That Third Fleet would show up, force the Japanese to surrender, and take him home.

Another time, he'd imagined the *Akasuki* floundering in a storm. In the daydream, a Japanese sailor tumbled overboard. While the Japanese fretted at the gunwales, Charlie dove into the water and rescued him because all life is sacred. After fishing them from the drink, the captain was so impressed he released him and his comrades.

Ridiculous.

He wasn't important. He wasn't the star of the movie. And he wasn't getting out of this. His command, crew, medals, and almost all evidence of his existence had sunk to the bottom. He was a prisoner and would be until the end.

It turned his very bile into a burning acid.

It made him want to scream.

He told himself not to abandon hope, but he had to stop hoping for the impossible. Stop wanting to control what he couldn't. His new objective was to get himself and his men home alive. Japan was almost licked. They might not have long to wait.

Eventually, Morrison stopped sharing his own fantasies of escape and slouched against the bulkhead. Sweat poured off him.

They sat like this for hours. Plenty to talk about, but they were too drained to say anything.

The door opened. Lt. Saito entered and said, "Last stop, gentlemen."

The men removed the clothes the Japanese had given them and changed back into their uniforms, which the ship's laundry had cleaned and pressed. Then Saito led them to the bridge.

There, Charlie saw Kure, the industrial city and great naval base.

They'd reached Japan.

He shivered in the wind. The October climate was far colder here than in the Philippines.

Vast industrial buildings covered the land surrounding the harbor. A smoky haze hung in the sky from workshops and ship funnels. Warships lay in rows at their moorings, meatballs on their hulls. Showers of sparks spat from arc welders. Trucks crawled under massive cranes.

Uniformed workers and sailors labored on the great Imperial ships, filling the sound with the drone of machines.

"Jesus," Rusty said.

Charlie thought the same thing. After years of heavy losses and its economy being throttled by submarine warfare, the empire was far from licked. If Kure was any indication, the nation remained productive and committed to war. Tanaka had said every man, woman, and child would fight to their last breath for the emperor. Nothing short of invasion would end the contest.

A bloodbath that could go on for years.

BRADDOCK

CHAPTER SEVEN

DAVY JONES' LOCKER

The grating honk of the collision alarm blared throughout the boat. All four engines roared at full loading, giving everything they had.

The 1MC blared: *"Rig for collision! Rig for collision!"*

The engine snipes jerked their heads to Chief Machinist's Mate John Braddock, who growled, "What're you looking at me for? Secure the goddamn—"

BOOM

The world whipped sideways, throwing him into the air. He crashed down on his side, his breath leaving him with a gasp.

Okay, that hurt.

Steel plates jumping, the deck buckled under his body. Loose tools and gear clanged off the engines and bulkheads. The engines whined and then screamed before dying one by one with a strangled whir and plume of acrid smoke.

The watertight door at the compartment's forward end slammed shut.

"What the hell happened?" Leach shouted.

Braddock glared at him. What did he *think* happened? Hint: The captain had thrown the *Sandtiger* in front of multiple destroyers to take on the *Yamato*. Which was crazy even for Harrison, though the man had the luck of the Irish.

Now, that luck had run out. One of those ships had decided to knock the *Sandtiger* on her can. And as Braddock had predicted, Harrison's luck running out meant everybody's time was up.

He pushed himself up. "Who's hurt? Anybody hurt?"

The deck tilted. He staggered but righted himself, his strong sea legs accustomed to balancing in heavy seas. Then he staggered as the stern sank.

"This is bad," he said as he lost his footing. Men and gear tumbled and crashed against the aft bulkhead in an avalanche of flesh and metal.

He shook his head to clear it. The lighting flickered before winking off, plunging the compartment into darkness.

"Turn on the fucking lights," he snarled.

The boat had been hit. She had no propulsion and was sinking by the stern. He knew to take these problems one at a time. Light came first.

"I think my arm's broken," somebody moaned. It sounded like Leach.

"Hang tight. Can anybody reach the lights?"

No answer. The boat hung dead in the water at a forty-five-degree angle. He'd have to climb up and do it himself, just like everything else in this department.

The emergency lights clicked on. Always the eager beaver, Petty Officer Third Class Gentry waved at him from the switch. "I got it, Chief!"

"Good for you." Braddock surveyed the pale faces in the pile of bodies crammed against the bulkhead. The men were gasping, but otherwise, it was eerily quiet.

No, not entirely quiet. An ominous rushing sound filled the air.

He hauled himself to his feet and gazed through the open aft passageway. Seawater was gushing into the aft engine compartment. Bodies and garbage floated on the oily deluge, which surged around the flooded engines. The boat groaned under the stress, the sound hollow.

"Christopher Columbus," he breathed.

Spray already moistening his skin, the sea boiled toward his compartment.

"Secure the door! Now!"

Estes helped him slam the door and dog it. Shaking, the sailor said, "We've been holed, Chief!"

"I know we've been holed, you moron."

Captain Harrison had finally gotten his suicide

35

mission. The arrogance of heroes. Captain Ahab was more like it.

He was likely still up there on the surface, shaking his fist at the Japs, gnawing on the *Yamato*'s hull.

While the *Sandtiger*, with negative buoyancy at her stern, headed straight for Davy Jones' locker.

"Hope he's okay," Braddock muttered to himself, wondering at the soft spot he had for the earnest lunatic.

"The guys in the aft room, they're all dead," Estes said. "They're dead."

Gentry had reached the sound-powered phone. "I can't get anybody, Chief!"

Estes moaned. "Do you think it's just us that's left?"

"Don't flip your wig," Braddock said. "Everybody forward should be all right."

"Well, what do we do?"

The boat was sinking without power, the phones were dead, and the engines were fried. One thing at a time.

Braddock spat and said, "We get the hell out of here."

CHAPTER EIGHT

DAMAGE REPORT

The engine snipes climbed the crumpled, inclined deck. With wounded sailors, it seemed to take forever. Braddock addressed everybody's whining with as much derision and sarcasm as he could muster.

He laid it on thick, playing the asshole. With a lifetime of practice, it required little effort and was worth it. For years, being an asshole had served to entertain him during the long, tedious hours of wage slavery the Navy called the submarine service. Now, however, it provided a far more important function.

Simply put, the more he played the asshole chief, the more his men believed they'd make it out of this alive, which helped them keep their wits and do their jobs. They were chuckleheads, but they were *his* chuckleheads, and he didn't intend to let them down.

Gentry led the way, helping to pull the

wounded up to the next handhold. The little eager beaver with the perfect white teeth was shooting for a medal. Let him. If they got out of this, Braddock would pin it on the kid's chest himself.

They reached the top. He tapped the door with a wrench.

Somebody tapped in reply.

"What is that, Morse?" Gentry said. "I think he's saying—"

Braddock banged again, hard. "Open the goddamn door!"

The sailors on the other side heaved it open. One peered out from the crew's quarters. "You guys all right?"

"Ducky," Braddock said. "Now get the hell out of the way."

"Sure thing, Chief."

"Let's go, swabbies," he told his engine snipes.

In the crew's quarters, the sailors off duty during the attack shouted questions from their bunks.

"Everybody, hang tight," he growled. "Somebody get Doc. I got wounded."

"I'm here," Chief Pharmacist's Mate Henry Pearce called from the far end of the compartment where he was sewing up a head laceration. "Anybody critical?"

"Broken bones and cuts, Doc."

"Asking again. Anybody critical?"

The pharmacist's mate could be an even bigger asshole than Braddock, who didn't mind. Any man who had to treat fifty-five sweating, filthy sailors for everything from mumps to VD to gunshot wounds automatically earned his respect.

"Nope," he said.

"Then they'll have to wait their turn." Pearce pointed at a bunk. "Put your men there, and tell them to wait."

"You guys stay here," Braddock told the snipes. "Those of you who are hurt, tough it out. Doc will be with you when he can. I'm going forward to see if I can get the dope from whoever's in charge."

He continued the climb, stepping over bodies until he reached the galley and mess. A-gangers worked on repairing leaks from ruptured hydraulic and air lines. The air was smoky here, a harsh chemical stink, but the fires had been put out. The deck was slippery, but the compartment wasn't flooding, a good sign.

Next came the radio shack and then the control room, where Spike was shouting orders at his men.

"What gives, COB?" COB stood for chief of the boat.

"Damage report, Braddock."

"The engines are broke dick for good. The boat's flooded from the aft engine compartment

39

all the way to the stern. They're all dead." And if they weren't, they had to take care of themselves.

Spike moved to the air manifold and cranked a series of valves. He was trying to blow the flooded compartments. "We were hit, and we're sinking. That's what gives. The captain gave the order to abandon ship."

Braddock glanced up at the secured hatch that led to the conning tower. "I take it we can't get out that way."

"The telephone talker opened the hatch to pass the order," the COB told him. "The idea was to evacuate one compartment at a time and save as many lives as possible. A second later, the boat just dropped from the surface, and Noah's flood slammed down on him. He secured the hatch, though. Saved our necks."

Braddock looked up at the hatch again and shivered. He pictured the telephone talker and the rest of them up there, lungs filled with water, floating in the ocean's eternal darkness. They didn't deserve that. People were assholes just as he was, but not in death. They left the world as they entered it, innocent.

He said, "We should try to refloat the boat."

Spike ran his grimy hand over his balding head. "The bow planes are on full rise. We're blowing ballast. All I'm doing is making the old lady sink slower."

"You're blowing the flooded compartments. That might do it."

"It's not doing anything. Can't you feel it?"

He was right. They were still heavy, getting heavier, slowly sinking.

"Why isn't it working?"

"My guess is the air and hydraulic lines are all smashed aft." He closed the air manifold valves. "All we're doing is blowing bubbles and putting a big fat target on our heads for depth charging."

"Give me some A-gangers, and we'll get right on it."

"The boat's barely holding together. We're still taking on water. We'll be vertical soon. The captain was right to abandon ship. The seafloor is 5,000 fathoms under our keel. I can't raise the boat, and if I could, the Japs would blow us out of the water. If we sink too far, this boat is going to be our coffin."

Braddock braced himself for more cheery news. "How deep are we now?"

Spike jerked his thumb at the busted depth gauge. "You tell me."

He looked around, still trying to think of a way to get the *Sandtiger* back on her feet. The COB was right. It was pointless. The boat was shot to hell. They had no choice but to abandon her.

Harrison had probably considered it a personal challenge to wreck the boat so bad Braddock could never fix it. Bash it up so he could look at Braddock and say, *We need all repairs completed so we can take another crack at the* Yamato. *Oh, and you have eight hours to do it.*

He chuckled at the idea. The sailors crowding the control room cast worried glances at him.

"That leaves Forward Torpedo," Braddock said. "When do we get out?"

"I'd say now would be a good time."

"You said the battle is still going on up there."

"Face the Japs, or get crushed in the deep. Take your pick. Now or never."

Braddock nodded. "Japs it is." A bolt of rage surged in his chest as he scanned the faces of the terrified sailors. "What was the Old Man thinking?"

Spike bared his teeth. "What did you say?"

"You gamble enough times, you always end up losing."

"Listen, you steaming pile of shit, the captain and a couple of outgunned tin cans charged the Japs to try to save our carriers from certain wipe-out. He fought off destroyers, shot his wad at the *Yamato*, and actually drilled some holes in him. The last torpedo circled back and hit us."

A circular run! Talk about your luck running out.

He said, "Okay."

"Okay? Okay? You sure you're done shitting on the Old Man? The man who respected you enough to give you your job?"

"I'm done."

"Good to hear it. Now get out of my sight and do the job he gave you before I punch your ugly mug into next week. Get the men to Forward Torpedo. I don't know how long I'm going to be able to hold depth. We're going down."

Braddock returned to the crew's quarters to round up the sailors for evacuation. God damn this war, where men had to die so others could live. And damn Harrison for going along with that lunatic math.

While Braddock had played the asshole to get through the war, Harrison had played it straight. He'd played the hero. He'd charged a battleship to save the poor slobs on a bunch of carriers.

It made him want to be a hero himself.

CHAPTER NINE

TOUGH MONKEYS

The sailors used blankets as stretchers to carry the worst of the wounded forward. Knowing the *Sandtiger* slipped deeper with each passing minute, Braddock yelled to keep them moving.

However, his usual charm failed to inspire the men now. Weighed down by fear and exhaustion, they plodded. When they'd been lying in their bunks, they could assure themselves the heroes were fixing the boat and would get them out of this mess. Moving meant summoning the courage to be heroes themselves because nobody was coming to save them.

To escape the dying submarine, the crew would have to swim for the surface.

"Get them out," Spike said when they marched through the control room. "Everybody. You hear me, Braddock?"

"I can hear you, COB," Braddock growled. "I'm right in front of you."

"Then move your worthless ass!"

He stopped at his locker to stow his shirt, shorts, and sandals and change into swim trunks and a skivvy shirt. The water would be cold but survivable, and he didn't want anything hindering his movement. Then he stuffed his beloved peaked cap, symbol of his rank and its status, in his shorts and strapped a bayonet to his leg.

Forward Torpedo was already crammed with men. Most sat on bunks and the empty torpedo skids, while the rest argued about how to use the Momsen lungs, which were underwater rebreathing gear. Braddock ignored them and found Dan "Guts" Buckner, the room's chief.

"How do you want to do this, Dan?"

"I was hoping you'd tell me," the chief said. "If you need a torpedo fired, I'm your man. Otherwise, I'm as lost as you are."

"Who's in charge then?"

Buckner gave him a quick once-over. "You're hired."

Braddock struggled to recall the escape procedures. Above the escape hatch was a cylinder-shaped chamber large enough to fit three men and a life raft. They'd be the first to make the dangerous journey to the surface.

"The first guys need to release a buoy and raft and tie them off," he said. "Everybody else will follow the ascending line up in groups of four."

"Don't tell me," Buckner said. "Tell them."

"I'm telling you. I need you to lead the first escape party up to the surface."

"Like I said. You need a torpedo fired, I'm your man."

Braddock sighed and yelled, "All right, swabbies, listen up! We've been pounding the pooch down here for almost two hours. We are going to polish this turd by making the most daring escape ever made by a submarine crew. Got it?"

Sweating in the stale, hot, humid air, the sailors stared at him.

"I said, 'Got it?'"

"Loud and clear, Chief," they muttered.

"Good! Do this, and you'll not only live, you'll be a hero! When you get home, you'll have dames climbing all over you against their better judgment. The COB volunteered me to get you sorry sacks off the boat, which means I'm last. I need three men to go up first. Who wants to be a hero?"

Nobody raised his hand.

He went on, "Don't make me pick three guys."

Nobody volunteered. It was useless. The sailors were brave, but none of them wanted to be first to attempt the swim to the surface. Nobody they knew in the Submarine Force had done this in a real combat situation. They hadn't trained on it since Submarine School, and they feared

47

failing their shipmates as much as confronting the ocean's depths.

Braddock glanced at Buckner, giving him one last chance, but the man looked away. At one time, the chief might have been called "Guts" for his courage, but the nickname had come to refer more to his expansive waist.

"Fine," he raged. "I'll go first. Who's going with me?"

Most of the men raised their hands. So that was it. They wanted a chief to lead them. A sea dog with long years on the boats behind him, somebody who knew what he was doing.

He would have laughed if it weren't sadder than it was funny. The chiefs had no better training or experience escaping a crippled submarine than they did. His brief stint in the escape training tank in New London felt like a lifetime ago.

This was what happened when you made men believe in you. He almost empathized with Harrison.

Braddock pointed at Gentry. "You there, tough monkey." He spied Boatswain's Mate Doug Whitley. "And you, Shorty. Get some lungs, a raft, and the buoy."

"Aye, aye, Chief," Gentry said and went to work.

"The rest of you work out three partners and get in line, nice and orderly. If you don't remember how to use the lung, ask somebody. Otherwise, I expect to see you all topside. If I don't, I'm coming back down for you, and I'll be pissed off."

Gentry handed him a Momsen lung. The mouthpiece connected to an inflatable rubber bag using two hoses, which had one-way valves for breathing in and out. A can of soda lime scrubbed carbon dioxide from the air, so it could be recycled. The same stuff the men were now throwing down on Forward Torpedo's deck to give them more time before the air became unbreathable.

He barely remembered what to do with the damn thing. It promised to work at depths up to 300 feet. He'd trained for eighty feet. If he made just one little mistake, he could suffer oxygen poisoning, anoxia, and decompression sickness. He could lose the line and end up floundering in the deep.

He didn't want to do this. He felt like a guinea pig in some egghead's lab.

"Good luck," Buckner said.

"I'll take balls over luck any day," Braddock replied. "Keep the men moving, Dan. It's on you now. Our last man taps the hatch, you drain the trunk and close the door, and then you send the next four up. Keep it moving. Got it?"

"Got it."

"Help Doc with the wounded. They're gonna be a problem."

"We'll be all right here."

"Good, because I can't do everything. I'll see you topside."

He took one last look around at the terrified sailors packed into Forward Torpedo, and his heart twisted in his chest. They were the same animal as him. Assholes to the last man, the lot of them. Tough monkeys. And yeah, innocent.

They were counting on him. He feared he'd never see them again.

Braddock mounted to the escape trunk. Gentry passed up the life raft, which he pushed to the side. Next came the buoy and ascending line, battle lantern, and hand tools. Then Gentry and Whitley squeezed in and dogged down the hatch.

The escape trunk's bulkheads surrounded the cramped space like a metal coffin. The 225-pound air supply valves were unlocked and tested. The oxygen lines blown. The regulator set at sixty pounds over bottom pressure.

Braddock knelt and undogged the trunk door that separated him from the endless ocean outside. The sea's pressure kept it sealed.

"Goddamn hero," he muttered, angry with himself.

Then he opened a valve to flood the chamber.

CHAPTER TEN

ASCENDING LINE

Cold seawater swirled around his feet. It rose to his knees and then his chest. As it compressed the air, Braddock breathed in and out to equalize the pressure in his lungs.

Gentry pinched his nose and blew to prevent ear block. "The water's at the top of the door, Chief." His voice sounded high-pitched in the increased pressure.

Braddock closed the valve to stop the flooding. Packed like sardines in the partially flooded chamber, the other men pressed against him, all elbows.

"Why'd you bring your bayonet?" Whitley said. "Are we fighting Japs?"

Braddock pulled his goggles over his eyes. "Sharks."

The sailor chuckled then frowned. "Do you think I could go back to—?"

"No." Braddock breathed deeply and held it, saving his Momsen lung for the ascent. He dove and shoved the trunk door. With the pressure roughly equalized, it opened with little resistance.

A murky and dark twilight world opened before him, and fear washed over him as he thought they were deeper than he'd guessed. A whole lot deeper.

It didn't make sense. If they were that much deeper, the door shouldn't have opened as easy as it did.

Then, here and there, he saw light beams brightening patches of water in his field of view. If he could see sunlight, the *Sandtiger* was within 650 feet of the surface. More like 200 feet from the looks of it. Must be cloudy topside. That or, more likely, black smoke had filled the sky.

He came up for air.

"How is it out there?" Gentry said.

"Freezing my nuts off." Braddock grabbed the buoy and spool of ascending line, and submerged again.

This was it. He was going to leave the submarine.

A rush of terror stole his breath, and he ran out of air quickly. He came back up coughing. He gasped, filling his lungs.

"You want me to go first, Chief?"

"Shut up, Gentry," Braddock growled and ducked into the water.

One thing at a time. Release the buoy, done. Pay out the line until it goes slack. Cut the line. They'd forgotten to bring up a diver's knife. He slid the bayonet from its scabbard and sliced it. Good.

Then he knotted the end around a pad eye at his feet. Perfect. He'd secured the buoy to the boat.

His triumph faded as he remembered the boat was still sinking. He'd given the line a few feet of slack in case he had to come up for air before he got it tied off, but he should have let it out farther.

Too late now. He wondered what else he'd done wrong or forgotten that was going to get him and everybody else killed. No wonder nobody else had volunteered for this lousy job.

He surfaced again, gulped air, and plunged back down to tie the raft line around the ascending line. This done, he released the raft. The bulky yellow package floated toward the surface on its own buoyancy.

Then he swam back up again.

"Everything's in place," he said. "I'm going up. Don't follow too close. I don't want to end up kicking you in the face."

"You'll float to the surface at a steady one foot per second," Gentry the eager beaver told him. "The men should be paced ten seconds apart."

"Sounds fine," Braddock said, good and terrified now. "I don't care."

At 200 feet, a rate of one foot per second meant three minutes and twenty seconds before he breathed fresh air again in sunlight. It promised to be the longest three minutes and twenty seconds of his life, but he could do it.

He had to do it. He had no choice.

Gentry pulled a hose from the air manifold, connected it to a valve on the chief's Momsen lung, and filled it. The bag expanded to a rigid block in front of Braddock's chest. Gentry closed the valve, checked his gear one last time, and patted his shoulder. He was good to go. Behind his goggles, Gentry's eyes were big and watery and wild.

The kid was terrified. The stupid idiot wanted to be a hero.

Braddock bit down on the mouthpiece and splashed under again.

After a few test breaths on the re-breathing apparatus, he hugged the line, remembering to drape his feet around it as well. His natural buoyancy started to take him up like a human elevator.

He floated to the first knot six feet up then the

next. At each knot, he was supposed to breathe in and out to adapt to the pressure and prevent decompression sickness.

He wasn't breathing at all.

He blew hard into the mouthpiece, almost spitting it out. A cloud of bubbles burst around him. Holding his breath too long while ascending was a terrific way to make his lungs explode. Who was the stupid idiot now?

Stay calm or die. That's what the instructors had told him back in New London. A simple enough statement, but there was something seriously wrong with it. If he went up too quick, he'd be dead. Too slow, dead. In the wrong position, yup, dead.

If his gear failed, if he lost his mouthpiece, if he let go of the line…

Stay calm. Sure thing.

In and out. Six feet. In and out. Six feet. Hail Mary, full of grace.

The groans of rending metal stirred the sea around him. Somewhere out there, a ship was going down, and the ocean's colossal forces were tearing it apart. Its death howl reverberated like an angry, departing soul searching for the Locker.

A strange, warm sensation crawled down his leg.

He was pissing himself in terror.

Anything to make your ride up more pleasant, Gentry, he thought and took a deep breath in and out in place of laughing.

So close now. The water above like a wavy sheet of liquid glass. He reached up—

And broke the surface. Still laughing as he tore the re-breather off.

Now using the inflated Momsen lung as a flotation device, he needed to swim aside without losing the buoy, or the current would sweep him away. He grabbed the line anchoring the raft.

And breathed deeply, inhaling fresh air, floating on sunshine.

Then a touch of decompression sickness hit him. His skin prickled everywhere as if covered in ants. His guts heaved, and he vomited into the water, which he splashed away with disgust.

Gentry came up next.

He'd panicked and lost his re-breathing gear. Decompression had burst every capillary in his face, covering it in a sheet of blood.

The kid started screaming.

Braddock reached out as the current carried Gentry away. Thrashing, the kid went under in a swirl of bubbles.

Braddock couldn't let go of the line to try to save him. If he did, he'd die too. Instead, he howled with frustration and fury as a squadron of planes roared overhead.

"You stupid idiot," he raged. "You see what happens to heroes?"

Braddock would take a big risk to save his men. Play a part to boost their morale. Lead them out of harm's way.

He wouldn't die for them. He was no hero.

"I'm sorry," Braddock said, his voice cracking.

Whitley burst through the surface. He wiped blood from his nose and grinned. "We did it! I can't believe it!"

Braddock rubbed his tearing eyes, blinking at the salty sting. "Did you remember to tap the hatch so the men know we're out?"

The boatswain's mate looked around. "Where's Gentry?"

"Did you tap the goddamn hatch?"

"Yeah, Chief!"

"Gentry didn't make it..."

The words trailed off at the sound of bombs and AA fire. The planes had reached their targets, a vast armada of Japanese ships that filled the view to the north. The ships were roaming in figure eights, absorbing strafing runs.

No sign of the captain or the other men who'd been topside. Then he spotted a man in the distance waving at him.

"Holy shit," Whitley said, pointing at the *Yamato*. "The captain went after *that*?"

"Help me get the raft inflated," Braddock growled. "There's a man out there needs help."

One by one, more crewmen floated to the surface. Most made it, though the sea swallowed a few who were wracked by the bends or weighed down by sheer panic. The exhausted sailors did what they could to save their brothers.

The warships crowding the northern vista turned and began to steam out of sight. Floating in the water and packed in the raft, the men watched them go.

The ships sailed over the hill.

Whitley broke the silence. "That all you fuckers got?!"

The sailors erupted in screaming taunts and insults. Some raised their middle fingers. Others beckoned the Japanese back to fight.

Behind them, the buoy tugged and plunged into the sea.

The *Sandtiger* and those still aboard had gone on eternal patrol.

CHARLIE

Miyazaki prisoner of war camp on the Japanese home island of Kyushu.

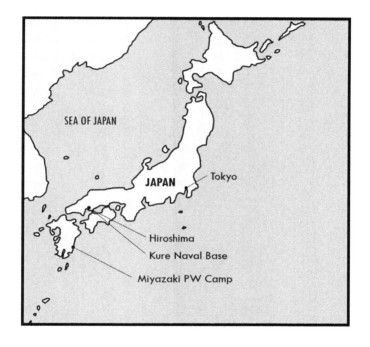

CHAPTER ELEVEN

BAPTISM

"Good morning," said the interpreter in charge of discipline. "*Konnichiwa*."

Charlie stared at the muscular soldier until a bamboo rod slapped the back of his skull. He stooped to approximate a bow.

"*Konnichiwa, Gunso* Sano," the Americans said in ragged chorus.

After disembarking at Kure, Charlie and his comrades had boarded a crowded merchantman bound for Miyazaki on Kyushu, the western-most of the Japanese home islands. The hellish ride down the coast was mercifully brief. Last night, they'd marched through cold rain until they reached Miyazaki Branch Camp, located two miles from the much larger prisoner of war base camp.

A naval guard unit, not the Imperial Army, ran the branch camp. It included an interroga-tion center.

They'd found the place eerily quiet. Sergeant

Sano had processed them as prisoners and warned against breaking the rules, of which there were many. Chief among them was no speaking at any time except when addressed by a Japanese.

The sergeant had issued them each a thread-bare blanket, toothbrush, tooth powder, hand towel, and dry clothes. They ate a brief meal of soup and warm rice before being marched into solitary cells. Charlie slept on a tatami mat on the floor until the guards woke him at dawn.

"Yoku yattane!" said Sergeant Sano. "Very good, pilgrims. You learn Japanese. You show respect to Japanese, any rank. Okay?"

"Hai," Charlie said with the others.

"You learn routine. You answer questions. You work. Most important rule is you do not speak unless answering a Japanese. Okay?"

"Hai."

"Any problem, you disciplined. You try to escape, you are killed." He tightened his grip on the *katana* sword on his hip. "Okay?"

"Hai."

Sano pivoted and bowed to the officer standing beside him. "This is Colonel Murata, camp commander. In Japanese, *taisa.*"

With his leathery skin and eyes narrowed to slits, the commander looked old enough to have served in the Russo-Japanese War. He murmured. The sergeant translated.

"He say, 'This is special camp for special prisoners. You are not prisoners of war. You do not receive privileges given prisoners of war. We rescue you from death. If you do not cooperate, we give you back.'"

Colonel Murata turned and began his slow walk back to the camp headquarters next to the guard barracks. Stunned, Charlie watched him go. The commander had just informed him that he would remain missing in action, presumed lost.

No Red Cross supervision of his treatment. No rights or privileges. Interrogation without boundaries.

Because he was already dead.

Beside him, Percy choked on a sob.

"Here is Lance Corporal Chiba," Sano said. "*Heicho* Chiba. Very friendly. He take you to *tenko*. Roll call."

Lance Corporal Chiba was a squat, pudgy soldier with round glasses and an ridiculous smile, like something out of a cartoon propaganda poster. A club shaped like a small baseball bat swung from his wide hip as he waddled over the cold dirt.

The man regarded the prisoners and chuckled. "More friends, eh? *Tokubetsu*."

Charlie nudged Percy. The Americans bowed. "*Konnichiwa, Heicho* Chiba."

The lance corporal sidled next to Charlie, put

his thick arm around his shoulders, and squeezed. "Good friend. *Ryokai*, Chiba-*san!*" He laughed. "*Iiko.*"

The Americans followed him across the yard to the barracks where other prisoners had assembled, about forty in all. Percy sobbed again. They were matchstick men, reduced by starvation. Faces bruised from violence. Ragged uniforms.

After the courteous treatment the Imperial Navy had given them on the *Akasuki*, Charlie had believed the Japanese might offer the same here.

He'd never been more wrong.

The submariners fell into formation with the other prisoners while Chiba, flanked by young soldiers with rifles, took roll call.

At the end, he opened a black leather notebook. The matchstick men around Charlie stiffened at the sight of it. Some of them were shaking.

He exchanged a glance with Rusty, whose eyes reflected his own mounting terror.

"*Keiotsuke!*" The lance corporal pointed at a man. "*Ichi.*" Then another. "*Ni.* Talking."

The men had apparently broken the no-talking rule.

Two guards stepped forward and yanked the Americans in front of Chiba, who chuckled as he slid his two-foot club from its thong. "Eenie, meenie..."

He reared at the American on the left.

And knocked a baseball out of the park.

The American collapsed like a house of cards, and that's when Charlie recognized him with a horrified gasp.

The man was a fellow member of the Silent Service. Lt. Commander Reilly, captain of the *Dartfish*.

CHAPTER TWELVE

INTERROGATION

Guards escorted Charlie to a small room with flimsy, bare wood walls and two chairs set at a table. Where he met Mr. Nakano. His first interrogation.

"Tell me about your hometown," the interrogator said.

As required, Charlie stood at attention during the questioning. "I'm from Tiburon. Near San Francisco."

Nakano was a young, handsome man with an easy smile. He spoke perfect English. Yale University, class of 1938. Worked as a general affairs clerk and interpreter at the Japanese embassy before the war. He wore slick suits and highly polished shoes. He was *gunreibu*, Naval Intelligence based at Kure.

"Never heard of that town," Nakano said. "Did you work there?"

"My father worked at the rail yards. He built

passenger ferries for the railroad. He died in a work accident when I was a kid."

He remembered the codfish canneries on the shoreline, the powder plants, the oyster beds, and the great trains. Like everywhere else, the town fell on hard times in the '30s. It was even harder for the Harrisons. Charlie's mother and sisters did their best to raise him, while he did his best to pitch in. He worked odd jobs in Tiburon and, when he couldn't find work there, across the bay in the mean streets of San Francisco.

Memories of the real world would get him through all of this. Now, he wished he'd taken the time to see his family when he was at Mare Island, just before boarding the *Sandtiger* nearly two years and a lifetime ago.

Men went through their lives with so many important things unsaid.

"So you joined the Navy as soon as you were old enough," Nakano said.

"That's right."

When he was a boy, the U.S. Navy used the coaling station on the eastern shore of the Tiburon peninsula. Charlie watched great warships dock under the giant cranes, and he fell in love. From the age of ten, he wanted to be a sailor. As soon as he was old enough, he joined up to provide for his family and see the world. He qualified as an officer candidate and attended the Naval Academy.

"Good," said Mr. Nakano. "Now tell me about Evie."

Charlie hesitated. "She's a friend."

Nakano removed from his pocket a wrinkled sheet of paper and unfolded it. "'My dearest Evie, I love you,'" he read. "'I'm sorry. Be happy.' There is no signature, but Lt. Russell Grady said it is yours. And yours, to Lucy, was for his wife."

Charlie remembered holding Evie's hand as they strolled down Main Street on a Saturday night. The carousing seamen and cannery workers swarmed the streets and gave the town a carnival atmosphere. The men crowded saloons, drinking in defiance of Prohibition or holding impromptu prayer meetings when word got around the revenuers were on the way.

At a rowdy baseball game hosted by the volunteer fire department, he kissed her for the first time.

He said, "Rusty and I kept letters for each other in the case the other was killed."

A sunny picnic on a hill overlooking the bay. They'd found an ancient native rock carving and wondered what it meant. *Men's Room*, she'd guessed. *Women's Lingerie.*

"Why did you write this to her?" Nakano asked.

"It's what I wanted her to know if I didn't make it home."

"I mean to say, why do wish to tell her you're sorry?"

She'd collapsed sobbing when he'd told her he was leaving to join the Navy. That he couldn't settle down until he'd ventured into the world and tested himself. It had broken his heart to leave her, but he had to go.

"Please mail her the letter," Charlie said, believing he was going to die here.

"I can do better than that," Nakano said. "I can send you home to her. But first, the war must end. Help me, and you can go home. You can go home to your girl."

CHAPTER THIRTEEN

MERRY CHRISTMAS

Nearly two months into Charlie's captivity, the guard kicked him awake at dawn.

Wrapped in his tattered blanket on his tatami mat, he stretched his aching body and rose. He folded the blanket and greeted the weak sunlight streaming through the window's wooden bars.

Outside, snow was falling. A good inch of it blanketed the frost-hardened ground. Charlie shuffled to the spigot on feet clad in wood shoes, where Rusty, Percy, and Morrison had gathered to wash.

Percy sagged with depression. Rusty looked determined to survive for his family but wasting away on the starvation diet. Morrison sported fresh bruises from interrogation and Lance Corporal Chiba's psychopathic attention.

All of them hungry and growing thinner by the day.

Charlie offered them a smile, which was his

only way to communicate without earning a beating. Rusty mirrored it, though it crossed his face for only an instant. Percy gave a glum nod. Morrison glared, his eyes burning with hatred for his captors. They shivered in the bitter cold, stomping their feet to keep warm.

Charlie had envisioned leading them in captivity, pep talks and plans, but that wasn't how it worked out. They lived in isolation, surviving at the edge. The special barracks was like a monastery dedicated to immolation.

Still, he hoped his smile conveyed their lone consolation; they'd all survived another day. One day closer to the end of the war and freedom. They just had to tough out today, and they'd do it together.

At least, he knew he drew strength from their presence. If he'd had to do this alone, without a familiar face, he might have given up. Rusty had his family, Morrison his desire to show the Japanese he'd never break. Percy seemingly had no such anchor and worried Charlie the most.

While Charlie's memories and thoughts of Evie tethered him to the real world, he'd worn them to the nub, and reality seemed further away with each passing day. As they'd lost their power to buoy his spirits, he found resolve from his comrades. He had to stay strong for them. That was his mission. He was still their skipper, and he had to stay strong.

The men gathered for *tenko*, and they studied Lance Corporal Chiba's face to read his mood. From what little Charlie could learn, B-29 Superfortresses had bombed Tokyo. America had her airbases in the Marianas up and running and would soon pound the home islands around the clock. Patriotic to the point of fanaticism, Chiba had become even more erratic and sadistic in recent weeks.

Charlie had grown adept at reading the guards and categorizing them as compassionate, neutral, or cruel in varying degrees. He'd learned plenty of Japanese but had become far more fluent in his captors' body language, which signaled whether a beating was coming.

Though rejects from the Imperial Navy and even the Japanese Army, most of these boys were professionally neutral, and some were even kind toward their prisoners. Only a few were predators like Chiba, swaggering around like Napoleon with his club and samurai sword, confusing *Bushido* with abuse of prisoners who could not defend themselves. Unfortunately, it took only one man like Chiba to create a reign of terror.

Today, however, Chiba seemed jolly as Sergeant

Sano made a rare appearance to tell the prisoners a big surprise was on its way.

A truck rumbled through the open gate a short time later. Like the usual vehicle that hauled supplies to the camp, it rattled at the edge of collapse, spewing black smoke from a charcoal engine.

A photographer stepped from the passenger side and took pictures as the driver pulled back a tarp.

Charlie gasped, his knees nearly buckling.

Oranges.

A massive pile of oranges, bright as gold.

"Go on, pilgrims," Sano said. "You may each take one."

Consisting of two prisoner barracks, head-quarters and guard barracks, interrogation center, and supporting facilities, the branch camp was isolated from the larger base PW camp. Only special prisoners came here, unofficial and off the books. Airmen, mostly, along with submariners, those the Japanese believed offered the most useful intelligence and, as a bonus, hated the most. To get the prisoners to cough up information, they were systematically broken down through abuse, which included living on half rations.

For breakfast, lunch, and dinner, the Japanese served gruel made of rice, maize, and soybeans, and it tasted like dust. Sometimes, soup with some carrot tops, potato peels, tofu, or fish in it. When Charlie first arrived at the camp, he'd suffered chronic diarrhea, squatting over a hole in the *benjo* multiple times a day until his body adjusted to the new diet. It barely sustained him, but there was no sugar or fat. Not enough calories to keep up with the aching cold, hard labor, and grueling calisthenics every morning. And not enough nutrition, leading to diseases such as beriberi and scurvy among the prisoners. Charlie had already begun to develop bleeding sores.

When he wasn't thinking about home or reliving the bitter loss of his command, he dreamed of food. Juicy steaks, fried eggs, chocolate cake, sizzling bacon, warm bread. As time passed, it grew to dominate nearly every waking thought.

Charlie lurched forward like an automaton, grabbing an orange and shuffling back into formation. His fingers kneaded the rough skin.

All the while, the photographer snapped pictures, and then he nodded to Sano and returned to the truck with his equipment.

The sergeant said, "Good! Now put them back."

The prisoners groaned. Some snarled like animals. The Japanese had used them for a propaganda stunt. The men wept as they returned the fruit to the truck, which drove away, leaving a choking cloud of smoke.

Lance Corporal Chiba chuckled and said, "Merry Christmas, Merry Christmas."

CHAPTER FOURTEEN

PROGRESS

"Tell me about your hometown," Nakano said.

Charlie crouched on the balls of his feet with his arms raised above his head. Pain shot through his ankles and knees. "You know where I'm from."

"Tell me about your hometown."

His legs trembled. It amazed him how ingeniously simple torture could be. Out of everything they'd done to him, he hated the crouch the most. "I already told you. Every week, for the past..."

He stumbled as he realized his brain couldn't recall how long he'd been here. Was it March? Had it really been five months?

And his hometown? He wasn't sure of that anymore either. He felt like he'd been born in this nightmarish place.

They hadn't let him sleep in days, handcuffing him in uncomfortable positions and punching him when he nodded off. They'd shaved his head. Sores from scurvy had opened in his skin, his joints had stiffened from malnutrition, and spreading paralysis had set into his legs from beriberi. They'd blindfolded him and rammed a club into his guts whenever Nakano didn't like his answers.

"I'll wait," Nakano said. "Until I get bored and order the guards to hurt you."

A stabbing twinge shot up his calves. His hands were numb.

"I'm getting bored," the interrogator said.

"Tiburon," Charlie cried.

"Do you think I like asking the same questions over and over? Give me something I can use! How many submarines are in your fleet?"

The agony was unbearable. "I don't—"

Nakano picked a handful of manuals off the table and waved them. "I know how your submarine works, Mr. Johnston."

Charlie had taken that name for a reason. The *Johnston* was the destroyer that had made the first move against impossible odds to delay the Japanese juggernaut. Every time Nakano said it aloud, Charlie drew strength from it.

"But that's all I—"

"Stop telling me things I already know," the interrogator shouted. "Where are your submarines operating? How are your submarine forces organized? What is your supply situation?

What new equipment did you have on your last patrol?"

"I already told you. It's—"

"Above your pay grade, right." The interrogator sighed with disgust and gestured to the empty chair. "Go ahead and sit."

Charlie collapsed to his knees. He pulled himself into the chair and sat, gripping the base out of fear he'd fall off. "Thank you."

So far, his officers hadn't divulged that he was the captain. His secret safe, he only had to put up with this baseline of abuse. He wondered what Reilly of the *Dartfish* was going through, what simple but ingenious tortures reserved for captains he had to endure.

"Let's take a break." Nakano lit two cigarettes and passed one over. Charlie flinched and then accepted it gratefully after he realized he wasn't going to be burned with it. Sakara brand.

"I'm sick of this," Nakano said.

Charlie took a drag and coughed. "I think we're making progress."

The interrogator laughed. "Let's talk man to man for a moment."

He was barely listening, savoring the smoke. "Sure."

"I think it's admirable you want to serve your country. I do. You have served her well. But my superiors want information, and I'll get it from you eventually. You know that, right?"

"No," Charlie said. "Even if I knew something, I wouldn't tell you. Ever."

"Why, man?"

"You made me a special prisoner. You told me I'm already dead. I would have started making up stuff to give you long ago if I thought it'd make any difference."

"You can reduce your suffering!"

Now it was Charlie's turn to laugh, but it came out as a dry cackle. "I will tell you one thing, Mr. Nakano, with all respect. If you hit somebody with a stick enough, they're going to tell you to shove your carrot up your ass."

He'd already decided, to beat Nakano, he only had to wait. Every week, more prisoners, mostly crewmen of bomber planes shot down over Tokyo, arrived at the special barracks. As fresh prisoners entered, those who'd been there longest moved to other camps. The interrogation frequency for the *Sandtiger*'s officers, meanwhile, had stretched from every day to one day every week or two. And any useful intelligence Charlie might have became useless as time went on.

As if reading his thoughts, Nakano nodded and ground out his cigarette. "Fair enough. Are you done with your cigarette?"

From here on out, the interrogation would become even more brutal.

Charlie took a final drag, held it in his lungs, and blew a stream of smoke. "I'm ready."

"Then let's resume our game." Nakano called out for the guard.

CHAPTER FIFTEEN

BAYONET DRILL

Midway through April 1945, Charlie woke at dawn. He folded his blanket, which was now infested with fleas, lice, and bedbugs. Shuffled outside to the spigot to wash. Visited the *benjo* to purge his dysentery. Lined up for *tenko*, listened to the men count off, *ichi, ni, san…*

He watched Lance Corporal Chiba pummel a B-24 Liberator pilot for an invented infraction. He ate his meager breakfast, gasped his way through calisthenics, and mopped the barracks.

The rising sun dispelled the morning chill. Patches of green on the muddy yard. Birds chirping. Spring in the air. A black-footed albatross glided onto the roof of the guard barracks and whistled. These birds followed ships around the Pacific, feeding off their garbage. Sailors once considered them good luck. Charlie smiled, reminded of the sea, his second home and one he missed as much as Tiburon.

With the arrival of spring, things were getting better. Interrogations were rare now. The horrible treatment designed to wear down the prisoners and compel them to talk had killed some of them. Following an inspection, a new medic had arrived, and he administered injections against dysentery and had arranged for a minor rations improvement.

As for Chiba, his attacks continued to grow more savage and unpredictable. Even this was a good sign, however. It meant America was winning the war. Bombers flew over Kyushu on a regular basis now. Several times, he heard the booms of naval bombardment. Third Fleet was off Japan's shores now.

Hope fluttered through Charlie's chest. The long winter was over, and after nearly six months in this hell, he was still alive.

The prisoners separated for work or interrogation. Rusty labored in the leather shop where he sat on a wood bench all day sewing ammunition pouches for the Imperial Army. Percy left the camp in a work party assigned to dig civilian bomb shelters. In February, he'd suffered a bout of hysteria and tried to kill himself, but the Japanese had sewn up his wounds so they could resume the pleasure of killing him slowly.

As for Morrison, the man's blue eyes, set deeply in his misshapen and bruised face, continued to smolder with hatred for the Japanese. He and Charlie worked in the sprawling gardens just outside the camp, a task that started at the *benjo*. Using a dipper attached to a pole, the submariners traded off scooping shit from the hole and filling a bucket.

This done, they detached the pole and used it to haul the bucket swinging between them. The gate guard held his nose and laughed as he waved them through. They trudged to the garden and dumped the night soil into a trough, where it would be treated before being spread onto the field. Here, the prisoners grew potatoes, tomatoes, carrots, castor beans, and daikons, which were like turnips. Then they lugged water out in buckets and ladled it onto the plants.

It was dirty, tiring work, but Charlie loved watching the plants grow, the change in scenery, this brief sanctuary from Chiba's random savagery. The idiotic simplicity of digging a hole and planting a seed. Taking his time mounding the earth as if this were some type of spiritual meditation. Here, in this tiny space between his hands, the world was beautiful, safe, and growing.

From the gardens, he could see the larger PW base camp to the west. Beyond that, power lines snaked down the Kyushu Mountains to the city in the north. Beautiful and ugly at the same time. Farmland all around.

By the end of the month, the first vegetables would be ready to harvest. Charlie hoped to steal some and share them with his crew, who were otherwise supplementing their diet by hunting rats, digging up worms, chewing on weeds.

On schedule, Japanese women wearing baggy pants or drab overalls hauled water along the road. Their men drafted to fight, these women continued to eke out a meager living in Kyushu's hill country.

An old woman stopped and fixed Charlie with her disapproving stare. Every morning, she eyeballed him on her way back to her village. The first time, Charlie had been embarrassed at his shabby appearance, but he'd shrugged it off. If she had a problem with how he looked, she could take it up with Hirohito.

This morning, the old woman didn't walk on. She approached the prisoners, who bowed among rows of cabbage. Her hand swept over the Americans as she yelled at their minder. The guard shrugged, argued back, then threw up his hands in frustration. By now, Charlie understood enough Japanese to infer the Americans disgusted her. He ignored her and returned to his work.

When he looked up, she was standing in front of him.

He bowed again. *"Konnichiwa."*

She pursed her lips and said something he

didn't understand. The guard watched and sighed through his nose. With a frown, she gestured that he should hold out his hands.

He did as she bade, and she gave him a baseball-sized lump of rice.

They stared at each other, Japanese woman and *gaijin*.

"Hmph," she said.

"Arigato gozaimasu, sobo," Charlie stammered his thanks. *Thank you very much, grandmother.*

The other prisoners in the garden gathered around. Charlie divided the rice equally and doled out the shares. He wolfed his, almost swallowing it whole.

He looked for the woman, but she was gone. Wheezing and banging on the ruts, a truck drove out of the base camp and past him into the special branch camp. When they'd finished their work for the morning, they returned to find the dilapidated vehicle parked in the main yard between the barracks. Prisoners crowded around it.

Charlie and Morrison broke into a loping jog, wincing at each step.

Sergeant Sano was handing out Red Cross packages. "Everybody take one. We're celebrating today."

The atmosphere was thick with tension. Something wasn't right. Rusty flinched as he took his package. Maybe they all thought this was just another cruel trick, though no photographers were in sight.

Charlie grabbed his package and scurried away, hugging it to his chest. He tore it open and studied his treasure. Tears quickly blurred his vision. Spam, corned beef, jam, chocolate, cheese, raisins, Wrigley's Doublemint gum, soap, Chesterfield cigarettes.

The prisoners melted away and headed back to their barracks. Again, that strange sense in the air. They looked terrified.

"Today is a great day for Japan," Sano said.

Morrison nudged him and pointed with his chin. Beyond the truck, Lance Corporal Chiba was drilling some guards in bayonet attack. One by one, the guards bellowed a war cry and charged to thrust against a dummy roped to a pole.

Except it wasn't a dummy.

It was the B-24 Liberator pilot's corpse.

Charlie groaned in horror and backed away from the grinning Sergeant Sano.

"A great day, pilgrim," Sano repeated. "Your president is dead."

CHAPTER SIXTEEN

SKILLFUL METHODS

"Why do you hate us?" Nakano asked.

Sitting in the chair across from the interrogator, Charlie hesitated. A new question. He had no rote answer for it and savored the change from the grating routine.

He'd learned to hate plenty of individual Japanese, Sano and the camp commander and Chiba most of all, but he didn't hate the old woman who'd showed compassion for an enemy. If he didn't hate her, he couldn't hate them all.

He chose his words carefully. "I hate Japan's military government."

"The State is the people," Nakano said.

"However you want to put it, you attacked us."

"However *you* put it, *we* were defending ourselves. Unless you think trying to dictate our foreign policy, cutting off our oil, and shipping weapons to China doesn't count as an attack. None of which was an official act of war, but practically was. We're fighting to survive as a nation."

"What I'm saying is the politics don't matter. We're at war."

"Of course. I just find it tiring how much brainwashing you've received. Worrisome, even. Propaganda so subtle you absorbed it long before your training. You refuse to acknowledge there might be two sides of this conflict."

"Actually, I'm worried about you."

Nakano planted his elbows on the table and rested his chin on his hands. "Why are you worried about me?"

"I'm ready to give you something. Information you and your high command do not seem to know or recognize."

"I'm listening."

Charlie's lips pulled back into a feral grin. "You're losing the war."

Nakano's face darkened. "Go on."

"You can't win. We have more ships, more men, more resources, better technology, and an endless will to fight. We have right on our side. We're going to wipe every one of your cities off the map. Invade Honshu with tanks and veteran troops. Fight all the way to Tokyo. And after we win—"

"Two million men," the interrogator snapped. "That's how many men we have under arms ready to die for the emperor. Behind them, 30 million civilian militia. You're wrong. We may not win the war, but we won't lose it."

"And after we win," Charlie pressed, "there will be a full accounting. For your government and the Nazis who started an evil war that killed millions around the world. The men who started this will be hanged. Men who beat prisoners to death will be hanged. Men who use the dead bodies of prisoners for bayonet training will be hanged. Men who torture prisoners will be hanged."

"Do you consider me a war criminal?"

"Hanged," Charlie repeated.

"You who sank merchant ships and left civilians to die in the sea in violation of the London Naval Treaty. You whose country dropped incendiary bombs on Tokyo and killed 100,000 men, women, and children in a firestorm."

"I did my duty—"

"The fact you were following illegal orders excuses you, is that it?"

"Did my duty, just like the pilot Lance Corporal Chiba murdered and used for bayonet practice. Just like the Americans you torture for information."

Nakano leered. "We use skillful methods, not torture. Torture is prohibited."

"Just like we don't execute war criminals. It's

skillful justice. During your trial, I'm sure you'll be asked why you hate us. You might even be interrogated with skillful methods first."

Nakano lit two cigarettes and handed one to Charlie. "I will miss our talks. You may find this hard to believe, but I get a little attached to my subjects."

Charlie froze mid-reach. "We're done?"

The man eyed him through a cloud of smoke. "Congratulations. My superiors are far more interested in your bomber squadrons than the war at sea. This was your final interrogation. After today, you're done."

From here on out, Nakano would apply his "skillful methods" to captured airmen. And Charlie only had to wait for the end when he'd have the final satisfaction of seeing this smug son of a bitch swing from a rope.

The interrogator rested his cigarette on the lip of his ashtray and opened a file folder lying on the table. "One last thing, though, before you go."

His cigarette burning forgotten in his hand, Charlie eyed the man warily. He wanted to leave now, bolt through the door, though of course he had no choice.

Nakano said, "It's about your patrol to the Sea of Japan."

"I already told you. We went there, we sank

ships, we came back. Captain Moreau was in command."

"It says here we destroyed two of your submarines in the same area that month."

"We were the only submarine in the Sea of Japan at the time," Charlie lied.

"Then it must have been your submarine that sank the *Roiyaru Maru*."

The name rang a bell, but Charlie's starved brain couldn't place it. "I don't know that ship."

"She was an ocean liner transporting elements of the 180th Infantry Division, Army of the Greater Japanese Empire. They were going to Manchukuo to join the Kwantung Defense Army."

"We found a convoy," he said. "It had two ocean liners in it. The other targets were passenger-cargo ships. We sank both the liners."

"Including the *Roiyaru Maru*."

He hesitated. "If that ship was there, then—"

"Do you recall shooting soldiers in the water?"

The name's significance jolted him. Charlie remembered the *Sandtiger* wading into the dying ocean liner's floating wreckage. Hundreds of Japanese soldiers and sailors huddling in crowded lifeboats or treading water. Men screaming in the dark.

A shot rang out. Then another. The enraged

Americans fired back indiscriminately with everything they had. The Bofors joined in with arcing tracer rounds, obliterating a lifeboat. Blood fountained from the boiling sea.

Cease fire, Charlie had roared at the sailors. *Stop your firing!*

"The soldiers shot at us first," he told Nakano. "The men fired back. There was confusion. Some of the shots went wild."

They'd hauled two Japanese out of the water and dumped them on the deck.

They attacked Pearl Harbor, Captain Moreau had gloated. *Look at them now.*

The interrogator smirked. "There's that brainwashing again. The fact of the matter is you murdered helpless, unarmed men. Twenty-two, it says in my report. Sinking the ship wasn't enough for you. You had to massacre the survivors."

"That's not true."

"What did you say happens to those who violate the articles of war?"

Nakano wasn't a tired bureaucrat interrogating prisoners on an assembly line. He was a keen professional who didn't give up easily, and he'd done his homework.

And in doing so, he'd won.

"Grady and Morrison weren't on the boat at

the time," Charlie said. "Percy was below decks and had nothing to do with what happened."

"And where were you?"

The only way to protect his men was to be honest. "I was on the bridge with the captain."

Nakano smiled. "And that, among your many other sins, makes you a war criminal by the standards of any nation, even yours."

CHAPTER SEVENTEEN

B-NIJU KU

The guards buzzed with the latest news. Adolf Hitler had shot and killed himself. Germany had surrendered to the Allies.

In the Pacific, the fighting dragged on.

Rise at dawn. Fold the flea-ridden blanket. Wash at the spigot. Fall into formation at *tenko*. Calisthenics. Eat a meager breakfast. Mop the barracks. Carry waste from the *benjo* to the gardens. Eat a few ripening vegetables when the guard wasn't looking. Pocket two carrots for Rusty and Percy.

The women marched along the road with their water buckets dangling from poles. When Charlie spotted the old woman, he bowed as he did every day now. The woman shook her head as she always did and walked on.

The shining sun warmed his skin. In Europe, the war was over. Weeks had passed since his final interrogation with Nakano. While he'd had sleepless nights over the *Roiyaru Maru*, nothing came of it.

The guard whistled. Lunchtime.

As they passed through the gate, a deep hum filled the air. The gate guards looked up at the bright blue sky. One pointed at the long white lines of contrails.

"*B-niju ku*," he said. *B-29*.

Niju, twenty. *Ku*, nine. *Ku* had another meaning: suffering and pain.

The Japanese forbade the prisoners looking up when planes were overhead, but Charlie snuck a glance. A B-29 Superfortress roared high in the sky, the sun gleaming along its silver fuselage. Even at its dizzying altitude, far above where Japanese interceptors and AA fire could reach, it was a giant.

The air raid siren didn't sound in Miyazaki, not for a single plane. This B-29 was only taking intelligence photos.

Laying the groundwork for invasion.

President Roosevelt was dead. The news had hit Charlie like another gut punch from Chiba. His captors told him somebody named Truman was now president. Apparently, Roosevelt had dumped Henry Wallace and picked somebody different to be his running mate in last November's election.

Whoever he was, the man had big shoes to fill. President for twelve years, Roosevelt led America out of hard times and into war. He'd given his country the New Deal and rallied its people after Pearl Harbor. For more than two years, the commander in chief had fought a global war on two vast fronts.

Charlie had worried the new president lacked Roosevelt's resolve to pursue the war until Japan's unconditional surrender, the only way to prevent America refighting the war in twenty years.

The steady flow of B-29s over Kyushu told him Truman was willing to go all the way.

In silence, the guards watched the Superfortress cross the sky, probably understanding their fate was sealed. The plane's mere presence contradicted the vast amount of propaganda forced down Japan's throat by its weakening military.

Seeing the great *B-niju ku*, hearing the news of air raids on Tokyo and other cities, the message was loud and clear. America was coming.

Even if you kill me, Charlie thought, *I'll win.*

Then Morrison chuckled and said, "Beautiful!"

Charlie gaped at him for speaking his thoughts. The gate guards wheeled with a collective snarl. Lance Corporal Chiba was already stomping toward him from across the compound. *"Nante iimashita ka. Keiotsuke!"*

Morrison stiffened to attention and bowed. Swept up in emotion, he'd made a horrible mistake.

Fury masked Chiba's face. He already gripped his club in one chubby fist. While he couldn't knock the B-29 out of the sky, he could vent his hatred on this American.

Charlie drew a deep breath and yelled, "God bless America!"

The words stunned Chiba.

"I think this is goodbye, Morrison." Charlie's voice cracked as he realized what he'd done. "You'd better get out of here. Good luck to you."

The corporal was screaming at him. *"Shizuka ni shiro yo! Keiotsuke! Keiotsuke!" Shut up! Attention! Attention!*

Charlie stood at attention as ordered and raised his hands over his head.

Redirecting Lance Corporal Chiba's rage had been instinctive. He'd known the brutal guard, who'd often singled out and pummeled Morrison for various infractions real and imaginary, would have killed him this time. Charlie had opened his mouth without thinking, but now he was terrified. His legs trembled and barely held him up as he waited for the first blow.

"Gomen-nasai, Heicho Chiba," he apologized, bowing his head.

"*Warui ko,*" Chiba snarled. *Bad dog.* Then he lashed out.

The club struck Charlie's shoulder, shooting a bolt of pain up his neck and into his brain. He staggered but remained at attention. Anything other than submission only earned a worse beating. The trick was to ride it out until Chiba grew tired or bored, if one could call that a trick.

The next blow cracked his head. The lights went out. He came to with his legs dragging beneath him, the gate guards hauling him up by the arms. His left ear rang with an impossibly loud, painful hum.

"*Keiotsuke!*" Chiba ordered.

More blows smashed into his arms, stomach, legs, knees, spine, head. He collapsed again, plunging into oblivion, only to be revived once more.

"*Keiotsuke!*"

Charlie spat blood and teeth fragments. He struggled to rise, his body refusing to obey, his vision throbbing with anguish.

"*Keiotsuke, kono yarou!*"

Hands heaved him to his feet.

The world spun before resting on a permanent tilt.

Chiba reared and swung for the bleachers.

Then the lights went out for good.

CHAPTER EIGHTEEN

FINAL INTERROGATION

"Why did you join the Navy?" Nakano said.

Charlie sagged in the chair. His recovery in the infirmary had taken over a month. Bedridden, he hadn't been able to exercise his legs to stave off the beriberi symptoms. Every part of him still ached as if he'd broken into pieces and been reassembled wrong. Even breathing hurt.

He had only a hazy recollection of what had happened to him. He was partially deaf in his left ear. Between his beating, the thiamine deficiency, and the scurvy inflaming his joints, he could barely walk.

He said, "I thought you said we were done."

For eight months, he'd suffered. He'd taken everything his captors had thrown at him. They could do nothing more to hurt him.

Because if they did, they'd kill him, and his suffering would end.

"Why did you join the Navy?"

It was hard to talk past the pain, which filled his every waking moment and colored his every thought. "I wanted to do my duty. I wanted to find out what I was made of."

Nakano said, "If I had a mirror, I could show you. You're meat. The rest is just a story you told yourself to make it all mean something."

Charlie stared dully at him and shrugged. His story may not have mattered to anybody else, but it still mattered to him.

"I'm sending you away from the camp," the interrogator told him. "One more duty to perform. One last chance to find out what you're made of."

Charlie struggled to sit upright. "No."

"Why does this upset you?" Nakano tilted his head, puzzled. "If you stay, Chiba will beat you again. He'll kill you. You know that."

"I don't want to leave my shipmates." He'd given up hope of making it home himself. If Chiba didn't murder him, the camp would.

"Not that you'll fare much better where I'm sending you," said Nakano. "Your story, my friend, is coming to an end."

So that was it. The "duty" the interrogator had referred to was his trial and execution for propaganda purposes.

Charlie set his jaw. "You want to hang me as a war criminal, go ahead. I won't sign or make any statement agreeing to your lies."

"You wouldn't be hanged. We'd cut off your head with a sword. But I'm not sending you to Tokyo for propaganda, though I admit that was my plan. My request was rejected. Instead, I'm sending you to China. Manchukuo, to be specific."

"I don't understand."

"A very important man wants to meet you."

Thoroughly confused now, Charlie gaped at him.

"General Okamoto, the Kwantung Army, has a long memory. He wants to meet the captain who sank the *Roiyaru Maru* and murdered his men in the water."

"Captain Moreau's dead. And Captain Harrison went down with his ship."

"It doesn't matter. The general wants to meet the captain of the *Sandtiger,* and I cannot refuse the general's request."

"Harrison and I stopped the shooting."

"It doesn't matter," Nakano repeated. "We are writing a new story. You are now Captain Harrison, who will atone for his war crimes in the Japan Sea."

"I won't play along with your crummy charade," Charlie growled.

The interrogator took out his cigarette case. "Now we come to the part where you do your duty one last time. If you don't go, I'll send

Lieutenant Grady." He opened the case and extended it to Charlie. "Cigarette?"

All this time, they'd played a game. Two actors in the same movie, speaking lines memorized from different scripts. At last, Nakano had gotten them on the same page.

His hand shaking, Charlie accepted the cigarette. The interrogator leaned across the table to light it for him. He drew deep and let it out. "I'm Captain Charlie Harrison."

He said it with relief.

"Good man," Nakano said. "You'll regret your decision once Okamoto gets his hands on you, but I admire your courage and sacrifice for your comrade."

"Speaking of which, I have a condition."

"You want your comrades moved to the base camp. That is acceptable. I'll arrange it."

"Thank you," Charlie sighed.

He'd often asked himself what he was willing to die for. The only certain answer he had was to save his shipmates.

It wasn't a hard decision to make. Like Nakano said, he was going to die anyway. Either Chiba or the special camp's brutal conditions would finish him before the war ended. The interrogator hadn't rewritten his story. No, he'd given Charlie the opportunity to finish his own.

To end his story with meaning.

"And I have a last request."

Nakano shrugged. He'd consider whatever Charlie asked.

Charlie said, "I want you to make sure my letter gets to Evie after I'm dead."

An air raid siren wailed in the distance.

The interrogator blanched at the ceiling. "If we survive long enough for me to send it, I will do this for you."

Minutes later, the ground shook with the thunder of thousand-pound bombs falling on Miyazaki from 30,000 feet.

BRADDOCK

CHAPTER NINETEEN

WAIKIKI

November 1944.

Braddock sat on Waikiki Beach, watching the idiots laugh and splash in the surf at the Royal Hawaiian. Past them, far out on the hazy blue, a submarine cruised the surface, returning to the war.

That's where Whitley found him, sitting on the hot sand, surrounded by empty beer cans, celebrating Roosevelt's re-election.

"Hey, Chief."

"Hey, what."

"I'm being reassigned. They're putting me on a relief crew."

Braddock shook the can in his fist. Still half full. He took a long swig of the warm beer and finished it with a belch. "Good for you, Shorty."

"Not when you hear where I'm being posted."

"Midway?"

"Yup."

"It could be worse," Braddock told him.

The kid could be Captain Harrison, rotting in a Japanese prisoner of war camp while sneering guards shoved bamboo up his fingernails.

"Yeah, I guess." The boatswain's mate fidgeted, pawing a groove in the sand with his shoe. "I just came to let you know and to say thanks for everything. I don't think I would have made it off the boat if it weren't for you."

Whitley would spend the rest of the war fighting boredom on Midway, drinking hooch made from pineapple juice mixed with 180-proof grain alcohol syphoned from torpedo motors. Why did a moron like Whitley live, while a hero like Gentry died? Why had Braddock lived?

He shook a few of the cans that were sticking out of the sand like *moai* statues. All of them empty. He had this dumb kid thanking him, and he was out of beer.

"You're welcome," he said. "Now get lost."

Thanks to Braddock leading the crew off the dying *Sandtiger*, Whitley would go on with his mediocre existence. Meanwhile, idiots on liberty would go on laughing and playing in the surf. The warships would come and go out there on the big blue, fighting their endless war. The world kept turning.

For three weeks, he'd tried to forget the horrifying isolation he'd experienced while floating to the surface. The terror of looking death in its empty face. The guilt of surviving while good men like Spike and Pearce went down with the boat.

Before the *Sandtiger* dropped into the crushing depths, the high-pressure air in the tanks had run out. The last men had to go up without a Momsen lung. They either ran out of oxygen along the desperate climb or ascended too quickly and got the bends, thrashing and screaming until the ocean dragged them back down.

No matter how hard he tried, he couldn't forget any of it.

None of which was Whitley's fault.

Braddock appreciated the honesty of guys who were openly assholes, but he hated bullies, drawing a fine but clear line between the two.

"Sorry, Shorty," he said. "Forget it. Take care of yourself."

The kid didn't answer. When Braddock looked, he found Whitley had made tracks for wherever the Navy had billeted him. Which was just as well because Braddock was the kind of guy who rarely offered an apology and had a way of making whomever he gave it to sorry he'd gotten it.

After the Japanese ships had turned and steamed over the hill, a destroyer found the *Sandtiger*'s survivors and picked them up. Then it was one debriefing after another, shuttling between ships until boarding a transport returning to Guam. From there, a bumpy flight to Pearl on an empty cargo plane.

Another debriefing at the Submarine Base along with accommodations at the Royal Hawaiian Hotel. He was rooming with the aristocracy now. He used to have to sneak onto the grounds to sit under the banyan trees, but now he was a chief petty officer and a hero to boot. With his pay bulging in his pocket, he toured Hotel Street, crowded with servicemen and MPs and bouncers. He ate at Wo Fat's and had two drinks, the legal limit, at Bill Lederer's.

At the next bar, Braddock met an IRS agent who said he calculated the brothels' tax base by counting towels sent through the local laundries and then multiplying by $3, the cost of a trick. This inspired him to walk to the Black Cat, located across from the YMCA at the end of the street, and stand in line until taking his turn receiving three minutes of loving attention from an attractive and efficient prostitute.

For the next two weeks, he repeated this routine, days sunning at the beach and nights carousing on Hotel Street, until he'd burned through his pay. And all the while, he put it off but could not put it all behind him.

Soon, his languishing would end. As with Whitley, the brass would reassign him. He could go back to the *Proteus* and work for Lt. Commander Harvey, who was only a slightly bigger fool than most, and wait out the end of the war.

While Harrison struggled to survive.

Even now, 4,000 miles away, the son of a bitch wouldn't let him quit. He was out there, suffering torture, while Braddock's biggest worry was catching a sunburn. With his captain held captive, Braddock couldn't take any satisfaction knowing he'd finish the war in relative safety behind the lines. If he did, Harrison would somehow win. Or Braddock would somehow lose; he wasn't sure.

The captain had seen something in him he didn't see himself.

Which made one of them an idiot. And given one, or both, a responsibility.

A shadow fell over him. He looked up, expecting Whitley, but instead, a yeoman gazed back at him. Behind the kid's head, the tropical sun blazed high in the sky.

The yeoman smirked at this big gorilla lounging on the sand in his swimming trunks, shoulders burned red and a wrinkled peaked cap perched on his skull. "You Chief Braddock?"

He sighed. "I might be. Who's asking?"

"ComSubPac is asking. Admiral Lockwood wants to see you."

CHAPTER TWENTY

WAR HERO

Sitting in the drab Navy office with Vice Admiral Charles Lockwood and Captain Avery Copeland, Braddock smelled a con.

Copeland was a public relations officer. A professional con artist.

"The loss of the *Sandtiger* is a major blow to the Submarine Force," Lockwood droned. "Yet Captain Harrison's attack on the *Yamato* may have changed the outcome of the battle and saved countless American lives."

"Yes, sir," Braddock muttered.

"Just as extraordinary was your heroic leadership in getting the crew off the sinking submarine. It's the first time it's ever happened."

"Spike Sullivan's the man you want to thank, sir. The COB. We wouldn't have gotten off that boat without him holding depth as long as he did. He died doing it."

The heroes of the *Sandtiger* had ended up dead

or captured, but everybody else kept trying to turn him into one.

ComSubPac lit a cigarette and studied him through the smoke. "You were the first to go up to the surface."

"Yeah. Sir."

"You released the buoy. Tied off the raft. Otherwise organized the evacuation."

"Yes, sir."

"Then that makes you a hero, son, whether you like it or not. Sullivan sacrificed himself to save his crew. You led them off. It's not a contest. You're both heroes deserving commendation in my book."

Restless and irritable, Braddock fidgeted. "Thank you, sir."

"I'm putting you in for the Navy Cross to go with that Silver Star I pinned on your chest after Saipan. Understand?"

"I'm honored, sir."

"I've been looking forward to talking to you but wanted to let you enjoy your liberty first," the admiral said. "I take it you're rested? Ready for duty?"

"I am."

"Good. Captain Copeland has a very interesting proposition for you."

Here it comes, Braddock thought.

Copeland leaned to the edge of his seat and smiled. "It's a real honor to meet you, Chief Braddock. Getting off that submarine was a hell of a thing."

"Uh-huh." Braddock didn't like the look of the man. Prim and proper, his platinum blond hair combed neatly to the side. Though a PR officer, Copeland didn't come across as smarmy or fake, which Braddock could have dealt with head on. No, the captain seemed genuinely excited to be in the presence of a war hero.

A true believer type. The worst kind in Braddock's book. The kind who fought for flags and ideals. Even Harrison had enough sense not to buy too much into all the patriotic floy floy.

"It's an inspiring story," Copeland gushed. He raised his hands as if framing a picture. "David and Goliath. One of the most decorated and successful submarines in the service makes a daring surface attack against the Japs' biggest battleship to save the invasion fleet."

"Until one of our crummy torpedoes circled back and sank us." That part wasn't so romantic.

"Stay with me here," the PR officer said. "Then after the *Sandtiger* goes down, you brought most of her crew back to the surface right in full view of the Japs. You paddled out with the raft and rescued a man from the gun crew."

"Who told me the Japs captured Captain Harrison and three other officers, while Admiral Halsey was off who knows where."

Lockwood cleared his throat in warning.

Copeland kept going. "And then when the Japs turned tail, you all yelled at them to come back and fight! You gave them the bird! Holy Joe!"

Whether Uncle Charlie was there or not, Braddock could only take so much of this nonsense before he showed his true colors. "So what do you want from me, sir? *Life* doing an article or something?"

The captain grinned, and his blue eyes shined. "I want you to tell your story to America on the Sixth War Loan Drive."

Braddock scoffed. "You're kidding me."

"We're rotating you home, son," Lockwood said. "For a very important service to your country."

"The *Sandtiger* went down in battle, but her crew survived, and so does her fighting spirit!" Copeland raved. "You'll go to the Big Apple and help rally public support so we can finish the fight. Put the axe to the Axis."

War bonds were loans given to the government to finance the war, and they removed money from circulation, which held down inflation. Americans could buy baby bonds for as cheap as $18.75 and redeem them ten years later for $25.

126

In Braddock's view, the rationing back home was bad enough. He thought the fat cats who were getting fatter off the war should be the ones paying. But that wasn't the reason he hated it.

"You got the wrong guy," he growled.

"I know you'd rather be out there killing Japs—"

"I figure I've done my fair share making dead Japs, sir. Me, I'd be all too happy to go home and let the heroes finish the job. That's the thing. I ain't a hero. The real heroes of the *Sandtiger* are either dead or rotting in a Jap prison."

Lockwood cleared his throat again. "This is no time for an excess of modesty, Chief. The home front is as important as the battle front. There are 130 million Americans fighting this war, not just the men and women in uniform. The war loan drives not only help us carry on the fight, they're good for morale."

"FDR just said on the radio the war is costing us $250 million a day," Copeland said. "Our goal is to raise $14 billion in a single month. Selling shares in freedom." Copeland's eyes flashed with excitement. "We've got Bob Hope, Kay Kyser and his orchestra, and Dinah Shore lined up. And now you. You'll put on your dress blues, tell your story, and march in a parade. Get your picture taken with politicians and Hollywood starlets and receive the keys to New York. Great stuff, huh?"

"Christ," Braddock said. Man, did they pick the wrong guy for this.

"We've got the Japs and the Krauts on the run. We're winning, but we haven't won yet. This is how we finish the job."

"You need a hero to sell bonds? Do something real, and get the captain out of Japan." He raised his hand before the PR officer could gush anymore. He turned to Lockwood. "He survived, sir. The Japs captured him. Right now, they're torturing him, and knowing him, he's taking it for his country. We owe him."

Lockwood squashed his cigarette butt into the overflowing ashtray on his desk. "I goddamn know all that already. What am I supposed to do?"

"I know you know where the camps are and that one of them specializes in submariners. Launch a commando raid, and get him out. Get them all out."

Uncle Charlie glowered as he lit another cigarette. "The only thing I know with absolute, dead certainty is you're going to follow your goddamn orders. Congratulations, Chief. You're going stateside. I expect you to represent the submarines with your utmost charm and grace."

It was a forgivable error. The man simply did not know John Braddock. Charm? Grace? The chief was capable of neither.

CHAPTER TWENTY-ONE

ARMY VS NAVY

On December 2, Braddock found himself yanked from the tropics and dropped into the freezing wind at Baltimore Municipal Stadium, waiting for the Army and Navy to go to war.

Today, the battle would be fought on the gridiron.

Huddled under blankets on the bleachers, thousands braved the sub-zero temperatures to witness the event everybody was calling the football game of the century. The forty-fifth annual contest between the services.

Army Chief of Staff General Marshall was here. So were Air Forces Chief General Arnold and Commander of the Fleet Admiral King.

"I'm not doing this," Braddock said.

"You'll be great," Copeland told him.

"There are what, 30,000 people out there?"

The PR officer snorted. "Are you kidding? More like 65,000."

"I'm not doing this."

"You fought in an underwater boat, assaulted a coastal gun on Saipan, and led your men off a sinking submarine. I'm sure you'll survive talking to a crowd. Just stick to the prepared remarks this time. Think you can do that, Chief?"

Two weeks ago, he'd landed in the Big Apple sore and rattled from flying halfway around the world on cargo planes. Captain Copeland whisked him to Times Square to give his first speech in front of a six-story Statue of Liberty replica, surrounded by dancing girls, movie starlets, and a giant cash register that rang up total war bond sales. Braddock, who regarded this kind of tinsel patriotism as a giant con, felt like Alice in Wonderland.

Constantly on the move to belt out more speeches, meet self-important celebrities, give interviews to reporters, and shake mitts with fat cats getting rich off the war, he'd barely slept since. The *Sandtiger*'s attack on the *Yamato* was national news. Everywhere he went, girls batted their eyelashes and wanted his autograph, a frustrating thing for a sailor with no time or social skills to capitalize on the attraction. Thanksgiving came and went in a blur. Braddock felt like a traveling roadshow. He'd thought the whole thing would be a cakewalk, but this kind of work was every bit as much wage slavery as submarine service was.

Now this. A few remarks to tens of thousands of people to kick off the most anticipated football game of the year.

Braddock said, "If you have to give such a hard sell to something that's supposed to be great, maybe it ain't that great. Ever think of that?"

Copeland ignored him. His eyes flashed again with that manic light Braddock found both mesmerizing and grating. "Here come the cadets!"

West Point's gray-coated cadets had arrived on troopships escorted by destroyers. Following a massive band, they marched onto the field and formed up in perfect squares. "BOOM, ahhh!" they yelled in unison under the clear, frigid sky. "USMA, rah, rah! USMA, rah, rah! Hoo-rah, hoo-rah! AR-MAY!"

After finishing their famous "rocket cheer," the gray ranks broke and clambered up into their section of the bleachers.

Having arrived on boats sailed across the Chesapeake Bay, Annapolis' blue-coated midshipmen took the field next.

"Oh, and it's more than 65,000 people," Copeland said. "The game is being broadcasted on the radio. Millions will be listening. Great stuff, huh?"

"Killer diller, sir," Braddock offered in sarcastic agreement.

A GI limousine drove along the field's edge. Men wearing business suits and toting tommy guns rode on the hood. Three heralds in medieval livery raised trumpets and blasted a fanfare. The door opened to reveal Navy's mascot, a goat wearing a little coat.

Sailors dragged the reluctant animal by its leash over to Army's mascot, a mule, to "shake hands." Braddock empathized with the poor little bastard.

Uniformed men raised massive signs for the crowd to see. ARMY-NAVY GAME WAR BOND SALES. $58,637,000. Anybody who bought a war bond could get a ticket to the big game. Uncle Sam was raking in the dough.

"You're up," Copeland said. "Go get 'em, tiger."

Braddock stood in his dress blues and walked across the field to the microphone, which was set up in the end zone. "Um. Hello."

His voice boomed throughout the stadium. The crowd quieted to listen.

He took a deep breath and said, "I'm John Braddock, formerly chief machinist's mate for the *Sandtiger*. You didn't come here to see me, so I'll keep it short and sweet. By now, if you read the papers, you know all about Captain Harrison's heroic stand against the *Yamato* in the Philippine Sea. It was a hell of a thing, but that kind of heroics goes on all the time in this war. Everybody's giving their all and then some. The job ain't nearly done, so I'm glad you bought war bonds so you could enjoy this great American game. And keep America fighting."

He glanced at Copeland, who gave him a thumbs up. Braddock's eyes narrowed as he jumped script. "There are men from my boat in a Japanese prison right now. I didn't especially like them all that much. I mean, they're okay. You get to know guys when you live with them in close quarters. You'd like them a lot, though. They were the kind of guys who did heroic things like charge the *Yamato* to save American lives. Incredible movie stuff, only it was real. They had wives and kids and sweethearts waiting for them back home, and they went and did it anyway because it was the right thing to do. I don't know if I would have, but Captain Harrison, that's the kind of guy he is. Him, you'd like the most. So let me give it to you short and straight. I need you slobs to buck up so we can finish this war and get him home. He gave everything, now you can hand over twenty bucks. We're not giving up until the job is done, and it ain't just victory that's on the line. It's making sure this..."

He grit his teeth, biting back a choice word that popped into his sailor's brain. "It's making sure this war, this darn war, is finally over so we can bring all the boys home for good."

The crowd went wild.

In a daze, Braddock returned to his seat. "Go ahead and let me have it. I ain't selling your bullshit."

Copeland grinned. "I hate to break it to you, Chief, but you just did."

"The war's just a goddamn product to you, ain't it? Like selling dish soap."

"The home front is as important as the front line. These people need something to believe in. A story, if you want to call it that. Good versus evil. The $58 million this game brought Uncle Sam will put a hundred B-29 bombers in the skies over Japan."

"So we're all good, and they're all evil. You really think that?"

"It doesn't matter. You're moralizing about our moralizing. Our moralizing has a useful purpose. Yours doesn't."

"Fine. I'm done arguing with you, sir."

"Good." The captain checked his watch. "Come on, we have to beat it. We're due back in New

York tonight for another event on the war bond express."

"Captain, with all due respect, I sold your soap. Now I'm gonna watch this game."

Copeland ordered, threatened, pleaded, and then finally gave up.

The Army Cadets and Navy Midshipmen jogged onto the gridiron to deafening cheers. The Cadets won the coin toss and decided to kick off. The ball sailed toward the end zone, and the Midshipmen took it forward to the thirty-yard-line before the Cadets hurled the Middie out of bounds. For the entire first quarter, the ball turned over time after time, neither team making any real yardage, while the captain babbled about their upcoming soap-selling schedule.

"Can you quit your yapping?" Braddock growled. "There's a game on."

Copeland had almost made him miss the Middies executing a Statue of Liberty trick play in which the quarterback hides the ball and pretends to throw it while handing it off to a running back. Navy got a first down out of it.

"I don't really enjoy football," the captain said.

Braddock gave him the fish-eye. "What do you think we're fighting for over there, sir? You hate apple pie too?"

"I'm a big baseball fan—"

"I already know you don't give a crap about liberty, the way I'm pushed around. Maybe you're a Nazi spy."

"My admiration for Captain Harrison goes up every day," the PR officer muttered. "Because you're impossible to manage. I don't know how he did it."

"Don't say I didn't warn you, sir."

"I'm just doing my job. Without me, there is no war."

"That'd be a shame," the sailor said.

Copeland punished him with the silent treatment. Another big, fat shame.

In the second quarter, Army advanced sixty-six yards in six plays, and then Dale Hall ran the ball twenty-four yards for a touchdown. A successful kick between the uprights delivered the extra point, putting Army in the lead 7–0.

At half time, the midshipmen in the stands performed their traditional serenade of the Army mule while Braddock fumed. Army hadn't won since 1938, but it wasn't looking good. Navy had lost some good players to injuries in the first half.

Army blocked a Navy punt in the third quarter, resulting in a two-point safety for the Cadets. Now it was 9–0. The Middie defense strengthened after that, and then their offense poured it on, driving 73 yards for a touchdown. Army 9, Navy 7.

"We got this now," Braddock said. "Watch and learn, Captain."

"You think so?" Copeland was suddenly interested. "You up for a wager?"

Another fish-eyed stare. "You want to bet against Navy? Seriously?"

"You're a submariner, and I don't even like this game, but I still understand the probabilities better than you. How about twenty bucks?"

"You're on. Sir."

"It's just nice to see you get worked up with patriotic feelings about something. Enough to put your money where your mouth is."

"Army hasn't won since 1938. Last year, we crushed them, 13–0. Just get that money ready to hand—aw, *come on!*"

Army intercepted a pass that would have given Navy the lead, taking possession at midfield. The Cadets' quarterback handed off the ball eight times to some big bastard who covered the fifty-two yards and scored.

Army 16, Navy 7.

"I've got the money right here," the captain assured him.

As the clock ran out, Army rubbed Navy's face in it by bolting fifty yards through a snow flurry to score yet another touchdown.

"Son of a—" Braddock bit back a stream of choice words. "Mother!"

"Chief, you just bought yourself a bond to aid the war effort," Copeland said. "You'll thank me later."

CHAPTER TWENTY-TWO

FAT CATS

In New York City, Christmas decorations already adorned building facades, lampposts, and storefronts as the nation yearned for the holidays. Chief Braddock and Captain Copeland made it to Grand Central Station just in time for the next item on the grinding schedule, a big formal dinner.

They rushed up Park Avenue to the Waldorf Astoria, which had donated a suite in the Towers with a personal bar, grand piano, and glittering uptown view. None of which Braddock would actually get to enjoy, his gilded cage being of a different sort.

The moment he dropped his sea bag on his plush four-post bed, the captain checked his watch. "No time for a shower. We're already late."

"Who are we fleecing this time?"

"The Big Apple's Illuminati. Corporations, banks, media, politicians."

"All right."

Copeland eyeballed him. "All right? That's it? You're not going to bitch about it?"

"Why would I mind fleecing rich people? Now let's get it over with so I can get some sleep."

"Good idea," the PR officer said. "We've got a packed schedule tomorrow."

We'll see about that, Braddock thought.

In the mirrored elevator, he inspected his appearance. His face was stubbled with five o'clock shadow, and his dress blues were a bit wrinkled, but he doubted anybody would care. They wanted a piece of the man who led the *Sandtiger*'s crew back to the surface, like he was some aquatic Moses.

He wore his Silver Star, Purple Heart, and brand-new Navy Cross pinned to his dark blue blouse. The award ceremony had been a perfunctory affair. Uncle Charlie stuck the Navy's highest award on his chest and shook his hand. Then the admiral's chief of staff showed him out.

Lockwood didn't seem to like him very much. Maybe he wasn't such a bad judge of character after all.

Staring at his ugly mug in the mirror, Braddock practiced smiling.

"No need to scare people," Copeland said.

When the elevator doors opened, they walked into the great entrance hall, which led to the

Grand Ballroom. Gold benches rested against silver art deco columns reaching to an arched ceiling, from which sparkling chandeliers dangled. The green carpet hushed their footfalls.

So this was how the other half lived.

He sniffed. "What's for supper?"

"Whatever it is, you can bank on it being amazing. This hotel has the best banquet department in the world."

"Great. I'm starving."

"We don't have time to eat, courtesy of your obsession with football," the PR officer told him. "You're on as soon as we get there. We'll have the kitchen rustle up something for us later."

Catering staff pushed the doors open for them, revealing another world that was even more opulent. Across the vast red-carpeted space, hundreds of fat cats in tuxedoes and evening dresses stuffed their faces at round tables. Interior balconies overlooked the floor. A cluster of massive chandeliers shimmered just below the high ceiling. Wait staff swarmed among the tables, serving dishes and pouring wine amid a deafening babble of gossip and business deals.

"Wow," Braddock said.

Forget Roosevelt and Congress. Forget the military. These were the people who ruled America, and this was where they met to talk about the ruling. You could cut the atmosphere of power in this place with a knife.

"Yeah, wow," Copeland said. "These are very important people. Don't let that chip on your shoulder screw this one up."

Whenever somebody in authority told Braddock not to do something, it always sounded like a dare. It just made the chip bigger.

He followed Copeland to a stage, where they sat in chairs facing the diners. A grinning, bloated glad-hander welcomed them on behalf of some philanthropic organization with a fancy name. Braddock let the captain do the talking, saving his strength for the trials to come.

The glad-hander walked to the podium and told his crowd of engorged philanthropists they were in for a real treat. The hero of the *Sandtiger* was here, battle of Samar, blah blah, blah. Braddock tuned it out.

Then it was his turn to speak.

He strutted to the microphone and tapped it. "Hello. Thank you for inviting me to give you some straight talk about the war. I don't know much about war, but I can tell you one thing. It's a racket."

Copeland groaned and shook his head. *Don't do it.*

Braddock did it anyway.

"I want to talk about a real hero," he said. "Marine Corps Major General Smedley Butler, the Fighting Quaker, the most decorated Marine ever. Decorated as in he won the Medal of Honor not once but twice. Not just brave, but smart—the smartest. Back in '34, he testified before Congress about a plot among the big industrialists to take over the United States government and put in a fascist dictatorship. If any of you were involved in that, I apologize for bringing it up."

The crowd murmured, restless and angry. This wasn't what they'd expected.

"In 1935, he wrote a book, *War Is a Racket*. In this book, he talks about how the Great War made 20,000 new millionaires in the US of A, all because of huge profits from the war. Men who never shouldered a rifle or fired a torpedo wanted war, they got it, and they got crazy rich off it. Twenty years later, America didn't want another war. But we had a huge trade with China and even more money sunk in the Philippines, so we pushed Tojo until he pushed back. Which was bad for the guys at Pearl but good for business. Manufacturers, meat packers, bankers—they've all made out great on the government's dime. The fat cats make the profits, the people get the bill, and a lot of good men are dead."

Braddock gave them his practiced smile. "It's

my job to tell America's poor slobs to buck up so you can make even more money. Which I did because we're in it now, so we might as well win it. Now I'm telling you it's your turn. You wanted a war, you got one, and you're raking it in. It's time to give some of it back to Uncle Sam so we can finish the job before even more Americans die for a war they didn't want. That is all. Thank you for your time."

Not surprisingly, nobody clapped. The Waldorf Astoria's Grand Ballroom stood silent, its hundreds of rich and powerful men and women struck speechless in their indignation. Their silence was all the applause Braddock needed.

The sailor stomped back to his chair and sat beside a very glum Captain Copeland. "I think I'm getting the hang of this, sir."

"Pack your bag," Copeland said. "You're going back to the war."

CHAPTER TWENTY-THREE

SAN FRANCISCO

The whistle blared at the Ford plant, signaling the day shift's quitting time. Dressed in grimy gray overalls with colorful bandanas wrapped around their heads and swinging their lunchboxes, women trudged out of the plant. The crowds broke up into smaller groups at each street corner until a woman was left alone.

She walked with her head down, the weight of the world on her shoulders.

Then she stopped and wheeled to face the man behind her. "What do you want, creep?"

Braddock froze, and not just because of her sudden fury. From her pegs to her big blue peepers, she was a genuine knockout.

She shook the metal lunchbox to show him she might redecorate his mug with it. "Well?"

"You're Evelyn Painter. You are, right?"

He'd seen her photo on the *Sandtiger* every time he had to report to the captain in his stateroom.

On a ship full of men at sea for months at a time, it was easy to commit a pretty female face to memory. Like a nomad remembering where the oases were.

Her eyes narrowed. "What's it to you?"

"I'm John Braddock. I served with your..." He didn't know what the hell to call their crazy half-on, mostly-off relationship. "I served with Captain Harrison. Aboard the *Sandtiger.*"

Evelyn Painter gaped at him, her chin trembling.

He raised his hands. "Now, hold it a minute—"

She started to bawl right there on the sidewalk.

Braddock wasn't any good at this, and he didn't have time for it. Soon, he had to catch another cargo plane to Pearl.

Where ComSubPac was waiting to string him up.

"Quit crying, will you?" The sight of it was killing him, not to mention drawing curious stares from people passing by. "I don't have much time. I came a long way to tell you there's a good chance he's alive."

She stopped. "The Navy sent me a letter saying he was missing in action. Joanie at the plant told me, when you got a letter like that for a submariner, it means he's probably dead. Presumed lost means lost."

"Not sub-mariner," he said without thinking. "Subma-ree-ner."

"What are you talking about?"

"That's how we say it in the service," he said, flustered. "Never mind. Forget it."

She gripped her lunchbox's handle tighter. *"What do you mean he's still alive!?"*

"I think the Japs took him prisoner!" he yelled back.

The girl teared up again. God, he was terrible at this. He told her everything he knew about the sinking, the Silent Service be damned. He was in plenty of trouble as it was. Adding some more made no difference to him.

The next thing he knew, she dropped the lunchbox and threw herself at him. He held up his arms in something like surrender while she clung and bawled against his chest. "Easy does it, lady!"

"I thought he was dead!"

"There, there." He patted her on the back. "Listen, doll. I don't want to get your hopes too high. I didn't see him get captured, and if he was, the Japs can be pretty rough."

She pulled away, fists clenched in anger. "Do you mean they're hurting him?"

"I'm sure he's fine." He couldn't bear another round of waterworks. Men, he could handle. Women, on the other hand, remained a mystery to him. He couldn't be his usual asshole self around the fairer sex, leaving him practically defenseless.

Evelyn wiped her eyes. "Thank you for telling me."

Braddock thrust his hands in his pockets and kicked a pebble into the street. "Well, you're welcome. I guess I'll be seeing you."

"Wait! You're leaving just like that?"

"I'm on my way back to Pearl. Got a plane to catch, or I'm AWOL."

After his speech at the Waldorf Astoria, the sooner he got off the mainland the better. Right now, he was probably safer being near the Japanese, regardless of what punishments Uncle Charlie Lockwood had planned for him.

"I barely ate my lunch today. You want half a peanut butter sandwich?"

"I wouldn't say no to it." Welcome in the USA or not, he was starving.

They strolled into a park and sat on a bench. He ate her sandwich and an apple while she pelted him with questions about Charlie Harrison, culminating in the one he'd dreaded: "Did he ever talk about me?"

"The captain and me weren't exactly bosom pals," Braddock told her. "To be honest, he was a real pain in my ass. Still, he was a good captain."

"He joined the Navy to find himself. Last time I saw him, the war had found him. It had really gotten under his skin, like it was becoming a part of him. It worried me to no end." She sighed. "Maybe you can tell me why a man can't find himself with a good woman."

"Um." Braddock had no good answer to that.

"And like a big fool, I just kept waiting right up to the day I got that horrible letter. And ever since. Because I am and will forever be in love with him."

"I joined up because of a girl I went to school with," Braddock said, more to change the subject than to make conversation.

"That sounds like a romantic story."

"Not really. Doris Kelly. She barely knew I was alive. After school was done, she'd found a job as a waitress. I put on my spanking new uniform and showed up at the restaurant where she worked, thinking, 'Wait 'til she gets a load of me!' I thought she'd see me as some big hero. I says, 'Remember me?' She says, 'Hey, George! Want to hear the specials?' That's when it hit me I was a stupid idiot."

Evelyn laughed with him, hers pleasant as music, his bitter as a stubbed toe.

"Oh my God," she said. "I am so sorry for laughing."

"It's all right. My pop was a mean son of a bitch. I probably would have joined up anyway as my ticket out of town."

"I heard you talking on *American Pilgrimage*." One of his radio appearances during the whirlwind blur that had been the war loans drive. "I'll bet if you went back, ol' Doris Kelly would see you in a whole new light."

Braddock responded with a glum shrug. "That boat sailed a long time ago."

"While I'll keep waiting for mine to come back."

He checked his watch. He had to get moving, which was too bad because he enjoyed this girl's company. Now having met both Evelyn and Jane, the tough Army nurse, he understood why Harrison couldn't make up his mind.

Still, he was eager to return to Pearl one way or the other. Maybe Uncle Charlie would bust him down to seaman, second class. Maybe he'd send him to spend the rest of the war in Whitley's charming company on Midway. He didn't care. He just wanted to go back. The bustle and babble of civilian life irritated him far more than the Navy's stupidity and grating routines.

He was a fish out of water in the real world.

She said, "You really have to go?"

"That's right."

"Thank you for telling me about Charlie, John Braddock. You gave me hope he'll come home to me, and that's everything."

He stood and dusted his trousers. "I just thought you'd want to know."

"Hey, John?"

"Yeah?"

"Before you go, I want you to promise me something."

"I'm no good at promises, but you can ask."

"Promise me you'll get my Charlie home."

Just like a dame, asking for the impossible. He was one tiny wheel in a vast war machine rolling across the Pacific. Unless he stole a yacht or planned to swim the whole way with a knife in his teeth, there was nothing he could do.

Despite all that, he couldn't refuse her. "I'll get the captain home. If there's a way, I'll find it."

"Good," Evelyn said. "And one more thing."

Defenseless! "Sure, doll. What?"

"Promise me you'll find a way to come home too, you big palooka."

CHAPTER TWENTY-FOUR

SPINNING WHEELS

The Navy reposted Braddock to the submarine tender *Proteus* at Pearl Harbor just in time to prevent Relief Crew 202 from blowing themselves up.

After stowing his sea bag in the locker under his bunk, he'd headed to the machine shop to re-familiarize himself. Tenders were floating bases for provision and repair. The *Proteus* housed a foundry, machine shop, and warehouse that stocked everything from radio transmitter tubes to toilet paper to torpedoes.

Sweaty men labored at lathes, presses, surface mills, welders, drills, and saws. Steel shavings littered the greasy deck. The warm, sticky air smelled like burned metal and lubricating oil. If the ship didn't stock a replacement part, the men could make one here in hours. If a boat being serviced needed new piping, the sheet-metal boys whipped it up. The *Sandtiger* had kept these guys plenty busy whenever she'd limped back into port.

For a gearhead like Braddock, it was like coming home.

A huddle of shirtless sailors behind the vertical boring machine caught his eye. He approached them wearing his winning smile. "And what do we have here?"

The men jumped, revealing a makeshift Gilly, which was a distillery designed to make torpedo juice. Its heat struck Braddock's face.

A sailor raised his hand and yelled, "Hi, Chief!" while another shoved his hands into his dungaree pockets and muttered, "Aw, shit."

His first day back aboard, and he already had to deal with chuckleheads.

The Navy knew its sailors swilled ethyl alcohol from torpedo motors. To discourage it, the Bureau of Ordnance added methyl alcohol to the ethanol. The sailors strained the mixture through stale bread to separate it. So BuOrd added croton oil. Since ethanol had a lower boiling point than croton oil, the sailors boiled it and captured the steam in a condenser, distilling it out.

"Turn that goddamn thing off," Braddock said.

"Sure thing, Chief," a sailor said and jumped right to it.

"You boys ought to be ashamed of yourselves."

Glummer now: "Yeah, Chief."

"I could smell the vapors all the way on the

other side of the room. Vapors that, by the way, are heavier than air and liable to sink right into your propane burner. I'm surprised you didn't blow yourselves to hell. Make sure it's properly sealed, and get a fan to push any escaping vapors away. Preferably somewhere an officer won't find it. Then we'll give it another go. All right?"

The men brightened. "Sure thing, Chief."

This act of leadership accomplished, Braddock went topside to take in the *Armorhead* lying alongside with her mooring lines doubled up. The refit crew was attacking the submarine's innards and hull with mops, chippers, scrapers, and paintbrushes. Next would come the more complicated repairs. And after that, if Relief Crew 202 wasn't too drunk, they'd take her out for a shakedown cruise.

The whole process of turning around a submarine took about two weeks.

A squat officer approached and leaned against the coaming beside him. "It's 'Chief' Braddock now, is it?"

Braddock recognized the man as Lt. Commander Harvey. "Yes, sir."

"Good to have you back, Chief."

"Thank you, sir."

"ComSubPac told me to take good care of you."

Braddock winced. "Did he mean it, you know..."

"Literally, or that I should put a bullet in the back of your head?" Harvey barked a laugh. "He was having a good chuckle when he said it, so my guess is he meant it in the literal sense. He seemed quite amused by some stunt you pulled off stateside."

Braddock blew out a sigh. "I thought my goose was cooked."

"Damned shame what happened to Harrison."

Harvey's dark expression suggested he meant it literally too. A Japanese prisoner of war camp was something you didn't wish on even your worst enemy.

Meanwhile, Braddock had gotten away with murder. He'd escaped the fat cats' wrath and was back safe and sound on the *Proteus*. Here, he could ride out the rest of the war far away from earnest lunatics trying to turn him into a hero.

Still, he couldn't shake the feeling he owed Harrison a debt, and he couldn't forget the foolish promise he'd made Evelyn Painter.

Unfortunately—or fortunately, depending on how one looked at it—he could do nothing about Harrison. Just a tiny wheel in a vast machine.

Over the next week and a half, the electricians rewound the *Armorhead*'s motors, serviced her big battery banks, and repaired wiring and equipment. Technicians inspected the periscopes and electronic systems. Storekeepers provisioned her with tons of food, munitions, and spare parts. Harvey took her out for a shakedown cruise and pronounced her seaworthy.

Meanwhile, Pearl buzzed with war news out of Europe. Though the Pacific Navy cared only about their war, something happened that was big enough to demand everybody's attention. As December wore on, the Germans had launched a massive counteroffensive, threatening to split the Allied lines. While the refit and relief crews serviced another returning submarine, this battle, which everybody was calling the "Battle of the Bulge," raged on the other side of the globe.

Aboard the *Proteus*, Christmas and New Year's came and went with plenty of assistance from the Gilly's moonshine. They sobered up in time for the Allies to break the German offensive and link up their broken line, dashing the *Fuhrer*'s hopes for an honorable peace.

Another submarine then another and another, while the war dragged on and on. Everywhere, the Allies kept winning, though victory remained elusive.

In mid-March, Braddock earned some liberty and once again found himself on Waikiki Beach watching the idiots frolic in the surf. Beer cans thrust in the sand. His peaked chief's cap on his head and his back burning red in the sun.

A shadow fell over him.

He said, "Take it somewhere else, buddy. Beat it."

"Well, well," a familiar voice drawled. "Y'all haven't changed one bit, have you?"

Braddock killed the beer in his hand and reached to crack open another. "What brings you to Hawaii, Lieutenant?"

The soldier sat on the sand beside him. As always, he was dressed in worn and patched Army fatigues. "It's captain now. But I thought I told you to call me Jonas."

Another crusader. This one had more scalps on his belt than Genghis Khan. Still, Braddock was glad to lay eyes on him.

"I see you made it off Saipan in one piece. Getting ready for another mission?"

"You could say that," Cotten told him. "In fact, it's why I came to see you, Johnny."

Braddock froze with his can half-raised. "What do you mean?"

"Seems ComSubPac took a shine to your idea about busting Harrison and the other PWs out." The Alamo Scout grinned. "You, me, and the Sixth Army Special Recon Unit, we're gonna make it happen."

.

CHARLIE

CHAPTER TWENTY-FIVE

GOODBYES

Charlie woke, folded his blanket, and washed at the outside spigot for the last time. Today, he would leave Miyazaki Branch Camp for good.

The beriberi had reduced his gait to a painful shuffle, but he moved slowly because he wanted to savor every moment. It was horrible, all of it, but it was real, and he was alive.

He wasn't just saying goodbye to his flea-ridden blanket but all blankets. Nor to the rusty spigot but all spigots.

To his friends who washed themselves beside him.

Getting to China meant he'd board a ship. He looked forward to again feeling the sea around him, so deep and full of possibility, and say goodbye to it too.

He breathed in the hazy air and coughed. The firebombing of Miyazaki had destroyed a quarter of the city. A vast wall of black smoke still hung in the northern sky. Ash still drifted down onto the camp like gray snow.

Rusty nudged him. Charlie stirred from his reverie and found his comrades staring back. They knew. They were going to the base camp where their chances of survival would be far better than here. He was headed to a certain and horrible death.

They bowed in the Japanese manner.

It was the only communication they could risk, though it spoke volumes. Choking back tears, Charlie returned the gesture, saying his final goodbye.

Sergeant Sano waited at the truck. Nakano leaned against it, smoking a cigarette and looking out of place in his neat business suit.

Wincing with jabs of pain, Charlie slowly clambered into the back. He gasped in surprise as Morrison climbed aboard and sat beside him.

"Lieutenant Morrison and I made our own arrangement," Nakano said. "If you don't survive the trip, he will take your place. If you do, he'll come back to enjoy special privileges at the base camp."

The *gunreibu* had taken out insurance on their deal. If Charlie had a change of heart and found a way to kill himself before submitting to General Okamoto's savage justice, Morrison would suffer in his stead.

He wondered what kind of special privileges Morrison wanted. It was an awful risk. Charlie didn't have to take his own life to die on the journey, which promised to be grueling. He was on his last legs.

As if reading his thoughts, Nakano said, "Don't take it so bad. You'll survive the voyage, and your comrades will survive the war."

"But you won't," Charlie told him.

The interrogator chuckled. "American grit." He lit a cigarette, symbolic of execution, and passed it to Charlie. "Enjoy it. It'll be your last."

Two guards climbed into the truck and sat facing him, rifles between their knees. Sergeant Sano patted the vehicle's side. The charcoal-burning engine started after a series of asthmatic coughs.

"When we win this war, I'll get my justice," Charlie said.

"Your war is over, pilgrim," Sano said.

As the truck drove away and Charlie took in Miyazaki Branch Camp for the last time, he spotted guards marching Rusty and Percy toward the camp gate.

Nakano was honoring their deal. Charlie prayed they'd make it home.

The gardens outside the camp thrived in the July sunshine. He bade them farewell too. And thanks for helping to keep him sane.

The truck trembled and bounced on the rutted

dirt track, sending bolts of pain shooting up his spine. Morrison embraced him and squeezed tight to keep him from toppling over. They passed a long column of ragged American prisoners from the base camp, marching toward Miyazaki to help salvage the ruins.

Then they came upon the women walking along the road with their poles and water buckets. Charlie smiled and raised his hand to the old woman who'd been kind to him. She stopped to stare, steadily dwindling as the truck gained speed.

He wondered if she'd survive. He wondered if any of them would.

Just before she dropped out of sight, she raised her hand in farewell.

CHAPTER TWENTY-SIX

THE TRAIN

The train pounded west then north along Kyushu's coast, heading to Fukuoka. There, a ship would take them to Manchuria, where General Okamoto of the Kwantung Army dreamed of his revenge against the *Sandtiger*.

Charlie had expected to be crammed into a cattle car with animals or materiel. His guards wanted comfort, however, so he found himself sitting on a bench at the rear of a passenger car. Japanese civilians had boarded the rest of the car, briefly eyeing the dirty, ragged Americans before sitting with vacant stares.

Across the aisle, the guards smoked and played cards. When they appeared sufficiently preoccupied, Charlie risked talking.

"You're a damned fool, Morrison."

"I could say the same of you, sir," the lieutenant said. "You took my beating. Then you volunteered for execution so we didn't have to go. You got us out of that place. I owed you this."

"You didn't owe me anything. You kept my identity a secret under torture."

Morrison grinned, revealing a missing tooth. "He got nothing out of me."

"You saved me far more grief than I got. And you protected the rest of the men fighting out there in the boats. You did your duty."

"Not yet I didn't. I still owe you a chance to escape."

Charlie's laugh turned into a violent coughing jag. Morrison eyed him with alarm and patted his back.

"Escape?" he gasped. "Where could we go?"

"I don't know, sir. But if the chance comes, I'm taking it."

"I did this so you would survive, not get yourself shot."

"Surviving isn't living. If you think I could live with myself after letting you go off and get killed on my behalf, you don't know me."

"For God's sake." Charlie didn't have the energy to argue.

They chugged through a ruined metropolis. As with Miyazaki, firebombing had leveled huge swathes of it. Here and there, the frames of solitary reinforced concrete buildings stood among vast fields of ash and rubble.

"Why don't they just surrender?" Morrison wondered.

"Would you?" Charlie asked him.

He respected their tenacity, but after everything he'd suffered, it was hard to pity them. They'd brought this horror on themselves. He might not live to see it, but he'd die knowing the men who'd dragged these people into this horrific war would pay, from Tojo to Nakano.

The train stopped at a station for passengers to disembark and board. Ash fluttered through the smoky air. Outside, the crowds looked hungry in their dirty overalls, bandanas tied over their blackened faces. The buildings that escaped the bombing and resulting fires were falling apart. Few vehicles were moving.

Still, the Japanese were busy, endlessly busy. Bombs had smashed the great factories, but Nakano had told him the people toiled in small workshops and even their homes, continuing to build bombs and bullets and war machines for the great struggle.

Charlie wondered what these people were thinking. Their once-proud empire was dying, their economy strangled, their cities in flaming ruin. They were one step away from famine and invasion.

He wouldn't be around to see the end of it, which filled him with regret but also, strangely, relief.

"I'm glad you're here," he told Morrison. "I still think you're a damned fool, but I'm thankful to have you along."

"We're in this together, sir."

"No, we're not in this together. But I'm glad I'm not alone."

"Sir, I have to ask you something."

"What's that?"

"What Nakano said about the *Ryoiyaru Maru*. Did it really happen?"

Through the window, Charlie spied a column of tanks and infantry choking a road that wound through the mountains. Two million men, Nakano had said. Many of them were here, digging in to meet the Americans.

"Sir?"

"Yes," Charlie said. "It happened."

Morrison grunted. Charlie guessed what the young lieutenant was feeling. Like Captain Moreau, he held to the simple maxim that the only good Jap was a dead Jap, but he was enough like Charlie to believe the rules of war trumped everything. Treat the enemy as you wanted them to treat you.

"What about you, sir? You were there?"

He remembered screaming at the men. *Cease fire, cease fire.*

He said, "I tried to stop it, but it doesn't matter.

Moreau is dead, but that's not enough for General Okamoto. Somebody has to pay."

On Saipan, he'd talked to Jane about karma. What you gave the universe, you got in cosmic balance. He'd cheated death while feeding it thousands of Japanese lives, but death always collected. The universe always righted its invisible scales. Simply put, if you lived by the sword, you were likely to die by it. Hate begot hate, passed on from man to man, an endless cycle of vengeance.

Maybe he deserved to die to, if nothing else, prevent him from taking part in this perpetual pattern. Because if he had to do it all over again, he might not give the order to cease fire. His suffering had become hate. If he had to do it all over again, he might pick up a rifle and join in. Kill every one of them, just as American bombers were doing every day from the skies.

He was starting to understand Moreau far more than he ever wanted.

CHAPTER TWENTY-SEVEN

THE HELL SHIP

A wide variety of motley *marus* and a few scarred destroyers crowded Fukuoka's harbor. These ships crossed the Japan Sea, still the Emperor's Bathtub, hauling troops and materiel between the home islands and China.

Standing on the deck of a rusting freighter, Charlie ignored the disheveled vessels as well as the smoke columns rising above the city. Instead, the glimmering blue sea held his rapt attention.

One of the camp guards shoved him. If Morrison hadn't caught him, he would have toppled like a bowling pin. Charged with taking Charlie straight to General Okamoto's doorstep, the guards were coming along for the voyage.

As for Charlie and Morrison, they were going down the hatch.

The heat struck them first. Then the stench. Then the moaning.

For the first time since Charlie had known

him, Morrison shuddered in fear. "Jesus Christ. What's happening down there?"

"Steady. We've made it this far. We can survive this."

They descended the ladder into the dark hold. The moaning grew louder. Charlie spared a downward glance and saw hundreds of writhing forms. Waves of heat and stench radiated over him.

At the base of the ladder, corpses lay on the deck awaiting disposal. Morrison stepped over them and helped Charlie, who was exhausted from the effort of descending the ladder.

Sitting or lying on the deck or packed into plywood bunks that were stacked against the bulkheads, Allied prisoners crammed the space. Many of them were dehydrated and sick with dysentery. Too weak to move, they soiled themselves where they lay. The decks were slick with human waste. The bulkheads seethed with cockroaches.

"Stay here," Morrison said.

Panting in the heat, Charlie fell to his knees among the dead. Sweat was already pouring off him. The foul air was thin and filled with mist.

"Captain!"

"Morrison?" he croaked.

The lieutenant returned gasping. He was shivering again, this time with revulsion. He kneeled.

"Grab me around the neck. I'll carry you on my back."

Charlie clutched the lieutenant, and Morrison grunted and pushed himself to his feet. He hauled Charlie across the deck of squirming bodies until he reached the bulkhead.

"I found you a bunk."

Charlie was about to say he didn't see an empty berth when Morrison hauled out a dead body and dumped it on the deck. In the cramped space, which was barely large enough to fit him, Charlie lay in the deceased man's filth.

The bulkhead hummed as the freighter started its engines.

"The ship's getting underway," Charlie said. Even though he was headed to his execution, it was a relief to be moving.

"The trip will be over in two days," Morrison said. "Three at the most."

"Don't let me die. Make sure I get there alive."

The man wasn't listening. Perched on the edge of the bunk and his face buried in his hands, his shoulders jerked with a sob. "Oh, God."

"This ain't nothing," Charlie told him, remembering Lt. Cotten's words from Saipan. Whatever Morrison had to deal with, it was temporary. Because it was temporary, it was only an illusion. "It ain't nothing."

"There's no end to it."

The horror, the suffering.

"You're going home, Morrison. You're the bravest son of a bitch I ever met. All you have to do is survive."

For Charlie, the end was coming soon.

"It just goes on and on," the officer moaned.

"You're going to go home and stay in the service and get command of your own boat. You'll make captain, I know it."

Morrison sobbed quietly.

"Tell me you're going to survive. That's an order."

The lieutenant wiped his eyes and took a long, jagged breath. "Sorry, sir. I forgot myself for a minute. I'm all right now."

Packed like rats in a cage with barely a square yard per man, the prisoners began to shift toward the ladder. The Japanese were lowering buckets of food on ropes. The prisoners' movement turned into a mad scramble.

Charlie opened his mouth to speak, but Morrison was already gone. He couldn't see what was happening past the mass of skeletal forms seething in the gloom. Voices shouted for calm, one of them Morrison's, countered by angry shouts. Some of the men fought with fists in a blind, mad frenzy.

Morrison shoved his way back through the throng and crouched in front of the bunk, holding out a ball of rice, which Charlie nibbled.

He wasn't hungry, a bad sign, but he forced himself to eat it.

The lieutenant wolfed down his own rice and offered a water canteen, which Charlie accepted gratefully. He took a long swallow. It tasted like rust, but he savored it. Then he handed the canteen to Morrison, who took his own pull and sighed. They shared it until it was empty, and then Morrison went to take it back.

The crowd settled quickly after the food was gone. The shouting and madness hung in the air like a psychic echo.

Charlie closed his eyes and shut it all out, retreating into memories he'd already tread thousands of times during his eight months of captivity. He hoped Nakano honored his promise to get his letter to Evie through the Red Cross. He thought about her, standing on tiptoes on Mare Island's piers and waving her red bandana over her head. He thought about spending hours in the dark with Jane Larson at the Royal Hawaiian, purging the war with wild lovemaking.

He'd often fantasized about a future with one, then he'd fantasized about the other, either a calm new beginning or restless roaming. Now, however, he pictured them living full, happy lives without him.

This fantasy carried him into a deep, dreamless slumber. He awoke to darkness and misery, men crying out in despair and thirst. Another mad scramble for a ball of rice and a canteen. More corpses hauled out along with the waste buckets.

Exhausted, he slept again. This time, he struggled with fever dreams of depth charges echoing in the deep.

Morrison shook him awake. "Something's happening."

Charlie raised his head. Was he still dreaming? Tremendous booms sounded through the water. The bulkhead trembled from the shockwaves.

The lieutenant wore a grim smile. "We're under attack."

CHAPTER TWENTY-EIGHT

TARGET

Whistles blared across the convoy to warn of submarine attack. The freighter's general alarm wailed. Feet tramped the deck above.

Charlie pressed his ear against the bulkhead. Metallic groans reverberated through the water. "We got one. It's sinking."

A string of depth charges banged in the deep. Then another sequence of deep booms at eight-second intervals.

Morrison jumped at the sound. "Our guys hit another one."

"We've got at least two boats out there," Charlie said. "Maybe a wolf pack, making a submerged attack."

PW ships typically had Geneva crosses on their hulls, the same red crosses hospital ships used. Squadron Commander Cooper had told him the Japanese didn't. As far as the submarines out there were concerned, this *maru* was just another merchant freighter. A legitimate target.

Another two booms in rapid succession, closer this time. Nobody cheered. The prisoners sat in tense, resigned silence.

The hatches above clanged shut. The Japanese had locked them in. If the freighter went down, they were dead.

Karma's last laugh at Charlie Harrison.

"Do it," somebody muttered in the dark. "End it."

Another string of depth charges.

Morrison directed his fierce gaze at the bulkhead above. "Kill them all."

More booms. Definitely a pack. They were out there, closing in on the convoy like sharks, tearing it to shreds.

If a full salvo hit the freighter, it would all be over in an instant. Either the torpedoes would kill him outright, or the cold sea would drown him quickly.

Regardless, death was imminent.

Charlie's breathed panicked gulps of air. "Morrison."

He clasped the man's hand. The lieutenant squeezed back as he too anticipated his demise. They wouldn't die alone.

"You're a hell of a submarine officer," Charlie said. "I'm proud to know you."

Morrison clenched his eyes shut. "I learned from the best—"

WHANG

The freighter reeled at the impact. The world lurched in the quake. Charlie's grip broke as a tangle of bodies consumed Morrison and tumbled across the deck.

Men cried out in the aftermath. Charlie rolled out of the bunk. The deck tilted toward the stern. They were hit. The engines had stopped. The sea was gushing into the lower holds.

The freighter was dead in the water and sinking.

"Morrison!"

The lieutenant staggered from the press of bodies. "Captain!"

Charlie pointed at the ladder. "Open the hatches!"

"What?"

"I can barely walk. You're going to have to do it."

Morrison squinted into the gloom and didn't move, no doubt wondering how he was supposed to accomplish his captain's order.

Charlie said, "You're captain now." The rank had become tribal, something passed down to the worthy. "You have to lead the men."

They were lucky only a single torpedo had

struck them. The freighter was taking on water and sinking, but they still had time. They all had a chance to survive if they worked together.

Soon, however, the American submarine would come back to finish the job.

"Aye, aye." Morrison hollered, "I'm going up the ladder to force the hatch open! We're getting out! Who's with me?"

Dozens cheered their approval. A surprising number didn't, choosing to give up and remain where they sat on the deck. After everything they'd endured, they welcomed the relief of death.

"You." Morrison pointed to a giant Marine. "This is my captain. The beriberi's got into his legs. Can you carry him?"

The Marine hauled Charlie into a fireman's carry. "Let's go, sir."

The prisoners surged up the ladder and heaved at the hatch until it broke. Charlie held on as the Marine grunted up the rungs. The brute lugged him topside and spilled him onto the deck before rushing off.

Charlie sat where he'd fallen, drinking in air and bright sunshine glittering on a bejeweled sea. Men were running in all directions. The Japanese were piling into lifeboats. One of the camp guards was there, shouting at the Americans. He fired his rifle at a man in the crowd, who went down in a spray of blood.

Spotting Charlie, he chambered another bullet and raised his rifle.

The prisoners swarmed over him in a frenzied pile. More shots rang out. Men screamed in rage and pain. The remaining Japanese leaped overboard to take their chances in the water.

Charlie struggled to his feet. Half the convoy was burning on the sea, whistles blasting in panic. One of the destroyers was almost vertical, its stern pointed to heaven, going down quickly in boiling foam. A distant ship exploded in a blinding flash, the shockwave nearly knocking Charlie to the deck.

The prisoners cheered and capered like lunatics, surreal against a vista of broken and burning ships. The general alarm continued to shriek its call to quarters. Two men held a sagging Japanese sailor between them while another bashed him to a pulp with a length of steel pipe. Others passed bottles of *sake* between them. An American pilot wearing the Japanese captain's peaked cap staggered past laughing.

Morrison emerged from the chaos. "The ship is ours! I'll get us some food from the galley."

"No time for that! Get life preservers. Anything that'll float. I'll meet you at the bow."

"Aye, aye!"

The lieutenant entered the mad throng. Charlie limped to the gunwale in time to see a torpedo wake streak toward the hull.

"MORRISON! We're about to be—"

BOOM

A massive fireball consumed the stern and mushroomed into the sky. The ship jumped in the water. The jolt flung Charlie into the air. Too terrified to scream or even think, he plunged toward the sea and landed in utter darkness. Chunks of the ship struck the water around him in angry splashes.

It was like the dream he'd had the night before he lost the *Sandtiger*. Floundering in a vast sea while Evie paddled toward him in a raft. He could see her now, smiling at him. She swept her hair out of her eyes and tucked it behind her ear, a simple gesture that always made his heart race. She beckoned. He couldn't reach. He was going down. Something dark and vast and primal lived in the sea, and it wanted him.

He stretched for her hand but missed. He couldn't do it.

Charlie lunged and gripped.

He coughed thick liquid. Evie was gone. He was blind. Whatever he'd grabbed onto felt slippery but solid in his hands, and it kept him afloat.

He wiped at his eyes. They stung, but he could now see a painful blur.

Oil. He was covered in oil.

He was clinging to a plank at the edge of an oil slick. Flames roared from the dying freighter in waves of steam and black smoke. Men screamed for help. The dead littered the slick, a floating carpet of bodies.

He paddled away as quickly as his weakened legs would take him. It was only a matter of time before the sea caught fire and consumed him with it.

Another freighter chugged close by to pick up Japanese sailors. Hoping for rescue, some of the surviving prisoners swam toward the boat. Rifles cracked as Japanese sailors shot at them. Others used poles to push the prisoners underwater.

A torpedo wake rushed past him. Charlie kicked as hard as he could, struggling to distance himself from the inevitable—

BOOM

The torpedo struck the freighter's bow.

BOOM

Another shot struck it amidships. Charlie's eardrums popped in the hot shockwave. Metal shards tore through the air with high-pitched whirs, thrashing the water around him like skipping stones.

The heat intensified as the oil slick caught fire.

"No," Charlie groaned.

He kicked through bobbing debris, willing his decrepit legs to move. Panting, he turned to see a lake of fire spread across the sea. Bodies, wreckage, floundering survivors, rowboats crammed with Japanese sailors. All of it went up in flames like a vision of hell.

Morrison had been right; there was no end to the horror and suffering. No end except death. The fire raced toward him.

And stopped. He'd made it out of the oil slick. He kept pumping his legs to escape the blistering heat.

When he had put enough distance between himself and the flames, he allowed himself to rest in the quiet aftermath. Charlie drifted alone on an empty sea. One by one, the convoy's great ships tumbled to the bottom.

Hopeless. Best to let the plank go and be done with it.

He couldn't. He didn't.

Not while there was still any chance at survival.

The sea in front of him exploded.

A gray submarine lunged from the water and leveled with a mighty splash.

CHAPTER TWENTY-NINE

HOMECOMING

Bloodied by its kills, the submarine appeared to stretch in the sun. Sailors rushed to stations on the deck.

Behind it, another submarine burst from the sea. Then another.

Charlie prayed they spotted him. With the world still a dim gray blur, he could barely see them.

So close to rescue now.

He shouted at the top of his lungs. It sounded weak and tinny in his oil-clogged ears. The sea wind swept his calls away.

One by one, the wolf pack started their engines with puffs of smoke.

"Help," he croaked.

Nobody heard him. They were leaving him here to die, karma's final spite.

No. The nearest submarine was turning toward him. The sleek gray shape grew larger by the moment. A security detail lined the deck with rifles and Thompsons. The captain stood on the bridge.

So close now he heard them talking about him.

"Why bother," somebody said. "He'll just drown himself like the other Nips."

"The captain wants us to try and get a prisoner. Throw him the line."

The line splashed nearby. Charlie grabbed on, but with his oil-slickened hands, he could barely hold it. They pulled him foot by agonizing foot through the water and hauled him aboard.

He landed on the deck in a black puddle. Two sailors aimed rifles at him.

"Christ, look at him," one said. "Skin and bones."

"Can't even feed their ship crews anymore."

Charlie gasped, "American."

"That's right, asshole. We're Americans."

"American," Charlie said. "Submariner."

The sailors glanced at each other.

A distant voice: "What did he say?"

"I think he's saying he's an American submariner, Captain!"

The other sailor: "They taught him to say that. Okay, Nip, you're American. Who won the Army-Navy game this year?"

"Shut it, Blackie," the captain said. "He doesn't

even look Japanese." He crouched beside Charlie. "I'm Captain Boyer. You're aboard the *Thornfish*. You're safe now."

Charlie nodded. "Good."

"Who are you, sailor?"

"Harrison. Lt. Commander. *Sandtiger*."

"What'd he say, Skipper?"

After a moment of stunned silence, the captain took a ragged breath. "Jesus Christ, it's *Hara-kiri*." He jumped to his feet and bellowed, "Get this man below now! And get Doc!"

"Aye, aye, Captain!" Sailors rushed to pick him up.

"You treat him like royalty, you hear?" Boyer said. "As far as you're concerned, he's Uncle Charlie, your mama, and the King of England all rolled into one." Then he shouted, "Wait! Commander, how did you end up here?"

"Prison ship," Charlie said.

The captain paled. "Ricci, tell Bryant to radio the other boats. We just torpedoed a goddamn prison ship. We need to look for survivors."

"Aye, aye, Captain."

"Godspeed, Captain Harrison. Doc will take good care of you."

They wrapped him in blankets and lowered him through the weapons hatch into the ward-room. Word had raced through the *Thornfish* their prisoner was a submarine skipper. Sailors came from across the boat to help. They propped him in a chair and crowded around.

"Christ, look at him."

"What'd they do to him?"

"He's been missing in action since last October."

"Isn't he the guy who went toe to toe with the *Yamato* at Samar?"

"Where'd he even come from? Is it true we sank a ship full of prisoners?"

"Make a hole!" A hulking officer in service khakis leaned in to inspect Charlie's face. "Yup, it's him." He smiled. "Welcome aboard, hotshot."

It was Bryant, with whom he'd served on the *Sabertooth*.

Charlie opened his mouth to speak. "Good..." He choked on the words as the crew babbled around him.

"Shut it, everybody," a chief growled. "He wants to say something."

"Good to see you, Bryant," Charlie said.

He gazed at his oil-covered hands and let out a wracking sob. He'd lost everything, Morrison was dead, and Rusty and Percy remained imprisoned. He'd suffered unimaginable horrors. He'd stared death in the face. But he'd survived, and he was here, among family, and he was finally safe.

At long last, Charlie was home.

Bryant swallowed hard, fighting tears, and rested his hand on Charlie's shoulder. "You're all right now. Where's the steward? Somebody get him some hot coffee and chow!"

"Doc's coming, Exec," a sailor called from the passage.

The pharmacist's mate pushed through the crowd and kneeled beside Bryant. "Commander, my name's Manning. You can call me Doc. I'm going to take care of you. First, we have to get you cleaned up."

"We got food on the way," Bryant said.

"Cancel it," said Manning.

"To hell with you, Doc! Look at him!"

"He's starving. I know you want to feed him, but if you do, you could kill him. He can have a cup of water, a cup of tomato soup, and some crackers, that's it."

"Hungry," Charlie said.

The sailors clamored to produce a feast. Steak, bacon and eggs, coffee. Whatever the commander wanted, he should get.

Manning pursed his lips at Bryant, who said, "Doc says no, and that's final." He glared at the confused steward. "Go get some tomato soup!"

"Aye, aye!" the man cried and hurried toward the galley.

"The next step is to give Commander Harrison

some space and dignity," the pharmacist's mate said. "Everybody, clear out and let me fix him. Exec, did I hear right that he knows you?"

"We served together on the *Sabertooth*."

"Then you can stay if you want to assist."

"Tell me what to do," Bryant said.

Wanting to help but having no way to do it, the sailors dispersed grumbling. With the room cleared, the pharmacist's mate went to work. He swabbed oil from Charlie's eyes, nose, ears, and mouth.

"See better now?" he asked.

Charlie nodded, so exhausted and bewildered he wondered if he was dreaming and he'd wake up clutching a board in an empty sea.

"You're lucky the oil didn't scratch your corneas." Manning gave him a shot, which he said was glucose. "Captain, just at a glance I can see you've got beriberi, scurvy, and the beginnings of jaundice because of the scurvy. I can help you, but you need hospital care. You also have serious injuries that may not be properly healed."

Bryant eyed Charlie with worry. "He's gonna make it, though, right, Doc?"

"Unless he's got even bigger problems I don't know about yet, I'd say yeah, he should survive long enough to get to a hospital."

Working together, they cut away Charlie's rags and washed the oil from his body with "pink lady," which was rubbing alcohol and other in-gredients, careful to avoid his open scurvy sores, which Manning treated with lotion.

Bryant stared at his scars in awe, some he'd gotten in combat and others he'd gained during his captivity. "What the hell did they do to you?"

Manning threw him a warning glare. "You don't want to know, and he doesn't have to talk about it until he's good and ready."

After cleaning the oil off, they washed him with soap and precious clean water. Then they helped him put on spare service khakis, which hung limply on his rail-thin frame.

The steward poked his head into the room. "Okay to bring in his supper?"

"Bring it," Manning said.

Charlie gaped in wonder at the bowl of hot soup and crackers set before him. He shoved a spoonful into his mouth. It burned his tongue, but he didn't care.

It was the most wonderful thing he'd ever tasted.

"He's got a smile on his face," Bryant said. "That's a good sign."

Manning touched Charlie's arm. "Take your time. Understand?"

Charlie nodded. Returning to the world had to be done slowly. One step at a time.

CHAPTER THIRTY

THE THORNFISH

After Charlie's small supper, Manning gave him a bunk and a mild shot of morphine. He slept for two days.

When he woke, he was ravenous, but that was nothing new.

The pharmacist's mate allowed him some buttered toast and water. Even this simple fare struck Charlie as a marvel, but it wasn't enough. All he could think about was fat and sugar. Cheeseburgers and apple pie.

"You're a submariner," Manning told him. "You know how to be patient."

Bryant brought him books and snuck him a doughnut, which Charlie tore apart in wolfish bites.

The captain didn't visit.

"He's still looking for more survivors from the prison ship," the exec said.

"He find any?"

"Nope. You're the lucky one."

"I'm the lucky one," Charlie echoed. He had to wonder about that.

Karma had a weird way of doing business.

As a result of having to adjust to a diet that was essentially new for his body, stomach cramps arrived soon after Bryant's visit. Charlie lurched to the officers' head to empty his bowels. Afterward, he wandered the submarine silent as a ghost while the crew eyed him. He guessed they'd been warned not to mug him until he'd properly recovered. No doubt, they were trying to reconcile the man who'd sunk the *Yosai* and taken on the *Yamato* with the hollow matchstick figure haunting their boat. In a way, Charlie was too.

It was strange being back on a submarine. Familiar yet alien. The *Thornfish* was a *Balao*-class boat, which were built with stronger frames and hull than the *Gato*-class submarines, enabling dives as deep as 400 feet. A step up from the old *Sandtiger*, a real beauty.

While its hum and diesel stench sounded and smelled like home, he didn't belong here. It wasn't his boat. He wasn't captain or even an officer here. Just a rider.

His home was at the bottom of the Philippine Sea.

By the fourth day, the trips to the head became less frequent and urgent, and Manning allowed him to eat bigger meals. His sores were healing. The pain in his joints abated a little. His decrepit legs gained strength. He had his first cup of hot black coffee, which he sipped like nectar.

A short time later, Boyer visited him in the wardroom. The two commanders regarded each other over burning cigarettes and coffee mugs. "I've called off the search. We've got new orders."

"Anything I can do?"

"You can eat supper with the rest of us officers tonight for starters. You seem to be back on your feet, more or less."

"And after that?"

He was tired of being in everybody's way, useless and taking up space. He needed something to do, even if Manning wouldn't approve.

"You're not ready for duty," Boyer said. "You're still sick as hell, and the way you yell in your sleep, you got some things to work out. Get better."

Charlie sipped his coffee, closing his eyes and savoring it. "If you have time, I'd appreciate you catching me up on the war."

"Since last October? Let's see, we took the Philippines. After that, Iwo Jima and Okinawa, the last military barrier to us invading Nippon proper. We bombed the hell out of Tokyo, flattened half the city with 700,000 incendiary bombs. Hitler's dead, Germany surrendered. Roosevelt died. Truman's president now, he's okay. And we finally sank your old friend the *Yamato*."

"Sounds like we'll be invading soon," Charlie said.

"Our heavy bombers are hitting their cities around the clock. Third Fleet is off the coast shelling them. More than sixty-five big cities have been firebombed. The next step is invasion, probably Kyushu first."

He finished his coffee. "I missed a lot in that camp."

Boyer winced as his imagination went to work. "You mind telling me what they did to you?"

"You don't want to know." It already felt unreal to him. "The Japs still have two of my men. Lieutenant Rusty Grady, my exec, and Lieutenant Jerry Percy. Lieutenant Les Morrison was also captured, but he was ... killed. Can you pass it up?"

"I'll let Pearl know."

"I also saw Lieutenant-Commander Reilly of the *Dartfish* at the camp. Pass that up too."

"I will."

Charlie felt a strange pull to go back to be with his shipmates, another to slumber in the deep with his command. "Were there any other survivors of the *Sandtiger*?"

"Thirty-three men made it off your boat. They were all picked up."

"Thank God." It was nothing short of a miracle.

"A chief named Braddock got them out."

"He's one of our best." If Braddock had died, Charlie would have heard no end of it from the chief when he showed up in Heaven.

"The papers made a big deal of it. The *Sandtiger* fighting the *Yamato*, the escape. Braddock gave some speeches last December as part of a war loan drive." Boyer leaned on his elbows. "Is it like the papers said? You charged, on the surface, straight into the thick of the Japanese fleet to buy time for our carriers?"

Charlie blinked at a blurry vision of the *Sandtiger* dying in the sea.

"Commander?"

He released the breath he was holding. "We fought off four destroyers, put two shots in the *Yamato*'s guts, and forced him off the line."

"A hell of a thing."

"Then our single Mark 18 did a circular run and nailed us in the stern. We went down quick."

The captain paled. "Jesus. The dope is a DD holed you."

"The dope is wrong."

"Well, what you did changed the battle, Commander."

Charlie shook his head. "The *Johnston* changed the battle. He started it all off. We just followed his lead and did our part."

"That was Captain Evans. Some of his men made it off the ship, but Evans himself was never found."

"The ship went down fighting." He remembered taking the ship's name as his own during captivity and how it had given him a deep well of resolve. "I owe him a great debt."

"How so, Commander?"

"It's a long story."

"There aren't many targets out there anymore," Boyer said. "Most of the Nip merchant fleet is on the bottom. Their navy's out of gas. We're one of several wolf packs in the Bathtub. Auckland's Avengers. With a name like that, you'd think *we* were taking on the *Yamato*. For weeks, we've been fighting coastal frigates and sampans. Auckland even worked up a few commando operations, sending parties ashore to blow up railroad tracks and the like. Then that convoy came along, something finally worth a torpedo. We really sank our teeth into it. Finally! I'd thought. Finally, some decent targets." He grimaced. "Then I find out I murdered hundreds of good men."

Charlie peered at him. "They don't mark their prison ships."

"It doesn't change the fact."

"I'll tell you something else you should know."

Interested, the captain leaned forward. "Yeah?"

"We wanted you to sink us. No, not because we're patriots. We wanted you to sink us because drowning in a Jap hold would have been a relief."

Charlie knew all about the kind of guilt Boyer must have been feeling. He wanted the man to know that, no matter how things turned out, the *Thornfish* had saved the prisoners aboard the hell ship.

"Well, we pulled you out of the water."

"You did. And I haven't thanked you yet."

"I've killed a lot of men in this war," the captain said. "Rescuing a fellow captain was probably the best thing I ever did."

Charlie understood that now too. So had Rusty, whose highlight of the war was saving downed flyers in Leyte Gulf. For Charlie, it wasn't sinking the *Yosai* or charging the *Yamato*, it was rescuing Jane and the civilians from Mindanao. It had taken him an entire war, and thousands of dead Japanese sailors, to discover this.

"Anyway," Boyer added. "Our patrol is coming to an end. We're going back to Guam for a refit. Not you, though."

"What do you mean?"

"New orders." The captain handed him a sheet of paper.

FOR THORNFISH X RENDEZVOUS SWORDFISH AREA TWELVE X TRANSFER HARA KIRI TO SWORDFISH X WELCOME BACK SON X COMSUBPAC SENDS X

Charlie wracked his brain to remember which stretch of water was Area Twelve. "That's the Seto Inland Sea. Why?"

"We're gonna find out," Boyer said. "You wanted to pitch in. Well, Uncle Charlie himself has something planned for you."

CHAPTER THIRTY-ONE

THE SWORDFISH

Submerged, the *Thornfish* arrived at the designated coordinates in the Seto Inland Sea and circled the deep, awaiting night.

After sunset, she prepared to surface.

In the crowded control room, Bryant turned to Boyer. "Ready to surface in every respect, Captain."

"Very well, Exec. Take her up."

Charlie stood by the TDC while the *Thornfish*'s crew expertly executed their surfacing procedures. His anxiety quashed any comfort he took in observing this all-too-familiar ritual.

The *Swordfish* was out there, already surfaced and waiting for him. He didn't want to leave. Despite his cleithrophobia, he felt safe in the bowels of the boat. Not quite home, but home enough.

The surfacing alarm bleated. High-pressure air blasted into the ballast tanks. The planesmen angled the submarine for her ascent.

Leaving the boat meant he'd eventually wind up back at Pearl. The doctors would pull him from the war for good. He didn't want that. He wanted to stay as close as possible to Rusty and Percy. He wanted to pitch in as long as he could to end this war. And he was afraid he could never truly go home.

From his hatred of the Japanese to his horrific nightmares, he'd feared becoming like one man. Reynolds, the S-55's XO.

How could Charlie ever function in the civilian world again? His life before the war seemed like a naive dream. Maybe he'd find Jane after all. She'd understand. He'd let Evie go for good. She'd be better off without him. Jane would soothe him. They'd caress each other's scars. They'd live for the day, running just one step ahead of yesterday.

The boat reached the surface. The quartermaster called out the all clear and added the *Swordfish* was nearby and waiting.

"Showtime, Commander," Boyer said.

Wearing a Mae West over his service khakis, Charlie climbed the rungs to mount the bridge. Still weak and easily fatigued, his sluggishness irritated him.

At the top, the cool night air was refreshing after living in the hot submarine for the past five days. The *Swordfish* lay at full stop a mere fifty yards to port.

The sailors ignored him while they rigged out a raft. They hadn't quite figured out how to treat the broken hero and regarded him as just another piece of equipment to be rigged and stowed as needed. Which was just as well.

The captain and Bryant mounted to the bridge. Boyer shook Charlie's hand with a firm grip. "Good luck, Commander."

"Thank you, Captain. I owe you my life."

"That might go both ways."

Boyer meant he'd chosen to regard Charlie's rescue as a redemption of sorts for his torpedoing a prison ship and sending 1,500 Allied servicemen to a watery grave. Charlie was glad to hear it. He didn't want to see the captain end up like Saunders, filled with regret.

"Take care of yourself, hotshot," Bryant said.

"You too, Bryant. Be sure to tell Manning thanks again for everything."

The sailors helped him into the raft and started paddling. As they drew near, the *Swordfish*'s hazy, black outline clarified in the gray moonlight.

She was a *Tench* class, the latest in submarine design, just introduced when Charlie last put to sea. She was about forty tons heavier than the *Balao* class and better built. Two five-inch deck guns. Twenty-eight torpedoes. And a ballast tank converted to fuel storage, which increased the boat's range from 11,000 to 16,000 miles.

Her sailors appeared in the gloom as the raft approached. One called down, "Hey, *Thornfish*! Did you bring that target you stole from us in the Bungo Strait?"

The chief rowing beside Charlie shouted back, "Sorry, we sank so many targets, we must have misplaced it!"

The men laughed, though the kidding was edged with real resentment. Targets had largely dried up, and more submarines than ever were operating across the waters once ruled by the crumbling Japanese Empire. Each was commanded by a skipper who wanted to make a name for himself before the war ended, creating a bitter rivalry among the boats.

"Here's our stop, Commander," the chief said as the sailors finished rowing beside the submarine. "Good luck, sir."

A hand reached down to haul Charlie up onto the *Swordfish*'s deck.

A familiar voice: "Miss me, sir?"

Only one man could make "sir" sound like "asshole" quite like that.

Surprised, Charlie looked up and found Chief John Braddock grinning back at him. "You know what. I actually did."

"Welcome back, Captain."

Braddock helped Charlie onto the deck. The *Swordfish*'s crew cheered as the chief enveloped him in a crushing bear hug.

BRADDOCK

The Seto Inland Sea between the Japanese home islands of Honshu, Kyushu, and Shikoku.

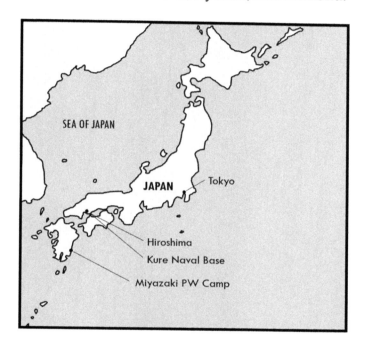

CHAPTER THIRTY-TWO

PROVIDENCE

Braddock released his captain quickly. He didn't want the man to get the idea he was going soft. Unsure what to say, he stepped back and fidgeted.

Though a natural cynic, he couldn't help but be amazed. He hadn't trusted the radio message about Harrison's rescue until he saw his captain with his own eyes. Even now, he hardly believed it. The whole thing was a miracle.

Captain McMahon broke the awkward silence. "Welcome aboard the *Swordfish*, Commander."

Charlie saluted. "Thank you, Captain."

McMahon returned it deliberately and with feeling. "The chief will take you below and spell things out for you. I'll be down directly."

As they made their way to the hatch, the security detail gaped at the hero of the *Sandtiger*. They reached out to pat the man on the back. Charlie flinched at the first touch. Then he grit his teeth and endured it.

In the wardroom, Cotten had poured three mugs of coffee and set them on a small square table that was bolted to the bulkhead.

The Alamo Scout stood. "It's good to see you again, Charlie." He offered a grim smile. "Though it's hard to see you like this."

Braddock looked away. It wasn't hard to see him; it was goddamn heartbreaking. Harrison looked dead on his feet. Rail thin, scars, chipped teeth, and more ghosts in his eyes than even Cotten had.

He couldn't imagine what the captain had endured.

Another miracle the man was even still alive.

Charlie shook hands with Cotten, who'd gone to hell and back himself and had the scars to prove it. "Good to see you too."

"The gang's all here. You turning up is like divine providence."

The men sat, and Charlie pulled his mug toward him. "Is anybody going to fill me in on what's going on? What are you doing on the *Swordfish*?"

"Admiral Lockwood sent us to bust you out of prison." Cotten snorted, smiling again. "But you being you, you had to come to us."

Charlie turned to Braddock. "They're still there. Rusty and Percy."

"What about Morrison? Nixon?"

He shook his head. "Gone."

Cotten: "How many Americans are at the camp?"

"There are actually two camps."

"But all y'all were held at the branch camp," the Scout said. "Special hellhole for submariners and airmen, right?"

"About fifty men in that one. More airmen coming in all the time. In the larger PW camp, I'd guess around six hundred. That's where Rusty and Percy are now."

Braddock glanced at Cotten, who responded with a subtle headshake. *Not now.* The chief scowled. If not now, when?

Charlie said, "So when are we going?"

"Not 'we,' Charlie," the Scout said. "My boys will handle this. We trained for two months for this op."

Harrison narrowed his eyes. Braddock knew that stubborn look well. Right now, the man seemed to be running on pure determination. One way or the other, he was going ashore with the commandos.

Braddock frowned. If Charlie pushed his way into the op, he just knew the earnest lunatics would try to talk him into coming too.

The Scout slid a large aerial photo across the

table. It depicted a series of buildings in an E shape. "You want to help? You can give us information. This is the camp as of a month ago. We know the layout, but we don't know much about the guards. How many, their quality, their schedule, that kind of thing."

"I'll tell you everything you need to know," Charlie said. "What's the plan?"

"On August fifth, heavy bombers are scheduled to pound Kyushu," Cotten explained. "The start of Operation Downfall, the invasion of the home islands."

"They're going to hit Miyazaki again, and hard," Braddock chimed in. "It'll keep the Japs busy while we make our move."

The Scout nodded. "We go in hard and fast just before dawn, get the prisoners out, and load them up on the *Swordfish* and two other submarines that will rendezvous with us in the Hyuga-nada Sea. Then we make tracks for Third Fleet and get you all to a hospital ship."

Charlie stared at Cotten then Braddock. "You can't fit that many prisoners on three boats."

The Scout sighed. "That's right."

"Just tell him, Jonas," Braddock said.

Charlie glared at Cotten. "You planned your op for the branch camp only."

"Yup."

"Rusty and Percy are at the base camp. How are we supposed to get them out?"

"You were always straight with me, Charlie. I guess I owe it to you to do likewise. The answer is I don't know. This is new information."

Overcome with emotions, Charlie was shaking in his chair.

Braddock eyed him with alarm. "We'll figure something out, sir."

"Yeah," Cotten said. "We'll talk more tomorrow. You should rest now."

The *Sandtiger*'s captain still glowered at them, intent on figuring it out now. Then he shook his head and sagged, suggesting a weariness set deep in his bones that he just couldn't hide anymore. "Tomorrow."

Braddock showed him to his berth. For the duration, Harrison would be hot bunking with the *Swordfish*'s officers. The chief fidgeted, and he was somewhat irritated he couldn't give the man any crap for almost getting him killed again when the *Sandtiger* went down. Harrison had been treated so poorly it wouldn't be right.

"I ain't tucking you in, sir," he said. "Good night."

Charlie sat on the bunk. "Braddock."

"What?"

"You did good."

"I wasn't about to let the Japs give you any more shit, sir. That's *my* job."

Charlie didn't laugh. "You led the men off the boat. I don't know if you got thanked enough, but now it's my turn."

"You're the big hero, not me."

"No." The captain's eyes blazed again. "I fought a ship. You saved the crew. Knowing you did makes me sleep a lot easier at night."

"I didn't save them all. So don't ask me how I'm sleeping. Good night."

"Braddock?"

The chief froze in the doorway. "Yeah. What?"

"Let me save the rest."

"It ain't up to me, sir."

"I can't go back without them."

Not *won't*. Not *didn't want to*. He *couldn't*.

"If there's a way, we'll do it. Good night, sir."

Braddock left fuming. For months, he'd built up a catalog of biting comments he'd hoped to unleash on Harrison the moment he saw him— just in case the captain thought Braddock went through all this trouble to rescue him because of any real affection. He'd even gone so far as to get Cotten to lie and say it had been all Lockwood's idea instead of his own.

Seeing Harrison in such a reduced state, unable to save his crew, however, robbed him of his instinct to be an asshole.

Lying in his own bunk in the nearby chiefs' quarters, he raged at what the Japanese had done to the man. What a single broke-dick torpedo had done to the *Sandtiger*. What Harrison had ultimately done to himself.

And what the war had done to all of them. Beneath all the flags and bands and Copeland's propaganda, the war was bloody, dirty, and horrific. A war fought between men who no longer saw each other as human.

Total war.

The *Sandtiger*'s captain screamed in his quarters.

Braddock hustled to the stateroom where Charlie slept. The man lay taut with terror on his bunk, sweating and moaning.

It reminded him of Harrison's fever after Saipan. Braddock worried about him then too. The captain thought fighting together was supposed to be some big bonding experience, like bowling. Yes, together, they'd sunk the *Mizukaze*, skirmished on Mindanao, and survived the horrors of Saipan. None of it endeared the man to Braddock, however. In fact, each episode only pissed him off more.

Seeing Harrison writhing in a fever at death's door, and now hearing him cry out in anguish in his sleep, this made him care.

The chief sat on the bunk's edge and squeezed his captain's hand. "You're all right now, sir."

Charlie's sweating hand gripped his back with surprising force. "Morrison!"

"You're on the *Swordfish*, Captain. You're safe here."

"You're a hell of a submarine officer. I'm proud to know you."

"I saw your girl in San Francisco on my way back from the bond tour," he said. Charlie was in delirium and couldn't hear him, but Braddock hoped the words would somehow get through. "Evie. What a doll. She made me promise to get you home." His face contorted into a wry smile. "Now I've got both of you making me dance to your tune."

Charlie stopped ranting. Braddock listened to his ragged breathing.

"Home," the man sighed.

"She's waiting for you, sir," the chief said. "All you have to do is get there."

CHAPTER THIRTY-THREE

THE BOMBING OF KURE

As days became weeks patrolling the Inland Sea, Braddock and Harrison, like the clannish Scouts, kept to themselves. Charlie slowly clawed his way back to life while no doubt fighting boredom and frustration as he rested and healed. Braddock stuck to the enlisted quarters, not minding his idleness one bit.

When he'd come aboard, the chiefs had been wary around him, worried he might try to stick his nose in their departments, but Braddock kept his nose to himself. The most important lesson the Navy ever taught him was to never volunteer for work.

Instead, he often sat on his bunk and played cards with his captain. They whiled away the hours in their games, old grudges and rank buried in the past.

Today, the game was Go Fish.

"Tens?" Braddock said.

Charlie handed over the catch.

Braddock inspected his hand. "Aces?"

"Go fish," said his captain.

Tension had risen throughout the boat. The Alamo Scouts paced like caged wolves, eager to be unleashed. In two days, heavy bombers would again fill the skies over Kyushu, and the Scouts would raid the Miyazaki PW branch camp.

Cotten figured his jungle fighters could take out the guards—a bunch of farm boys with no real combat experience—and liberate the prisoners at both camps. The problem was getting them all off the island.

Even if the submarines cruised on the surface with the prisoners cramming the decks, they couldn't all fit. And even if they could fit, they couldn't deliver them to the boats before the enemy responded.

Japan's high command had predicted Kyushu was the likely first target for invasion. Military units packed the island. Tanks, infantry, special units. The Japanese would mow them down on the shoreline.

The best option, it seemed, was to leave Rusty and Percy at the base camp.

Harrison said he understood, but he clearly didn't accept it. Braddock was honoring his promise to bring his captain home, but Harrison wasn't here, not really. A part of him was still in Japan, and he couldn't actually go home until the last of his crew was free.

But that wasn't how war worked. It was chaotic and uncaring. Harrison would be going home without his men.

"Kings," Charlie said.

Braddock passed one over.

"Kings."

Another card.

"Kings."

Taking his last catch, Charlie laid down his book of four kings. "Twos."

The man played cards the same way he went after ships, a bulldog chomping on the seat of your drawers and never letting go. Venting his frustration on the cards. The man should have been in a hospital, not sailing around Japan.

"Go fish, sir."

Captain McMahon entered and filled the small space with his bulk. "I've got news."

Grateful for the break, Braddock slapped his cards on the blanket. "What's the word, sir?"

"Come to the wardroom. Both of you."

Cotten was waiting there, glowering with folded arms. Whatever was happening, it didn't look good. Charlie and Braddock grabbed chairs.

McMahon remained standing, bouncing on his

heels as if bursting with his news. "Something big has happened. Third Fleet found what was left of the Jap navy at Kure. Halsey sent in two thousand planes. It was a total wipeout."

The Americans had destroyed an aircraft carrier, three battleships, five cruisers, and other ships, in addition to more than 300 planes.

"Why?" Braddock wondered.

McMahon looked down at him. "Why not?"

"The Jap navy wasn't a threat anymore. They were out of gas."

"By destroying their fleet, they can't use it as a bargaining chip. We want their unconditional surrender. Otherwise, they get complete destruction."

Charlie nodded with satisfaction. "Every bit helps."

McMahon said, "Again, why not?"

"Tell them the rest, Captain," Cotten said. "About scrubbing the mission."

"Now hang on," McMahon growled. "It's just postponed a bit. We received orders for a priority mission. We're to sail north toward Kure and hold station."

"That's it?" Braddock said. "What are we doing, looking for mines?"

The captain of the *Swordfish* answered with a jubilant grin. "We're going to observe and report on an attack that's apparently going to make the destruction of the Jap fleet look like child's play."

"What's the target?" Charlie said.

If the rescue of his men were to be delayed, he would of course want the wait to be worth it.

"Hiroshima, a coastal city."

"Never heard of it," said Braddock.

"The Jap Second Army is headquartered there, along with the Chugoku Regional Army and the Army Marines. It's a major port, embarkation point for troops, and depot for war materiel. There's war industry there, factories cranking out bombs, rifles, boats. Otherwise, I don't know why it's been targeted for this special attack. So far as I know, it hasn't even been hit by our bombers."

"We go and observe this attack," Charlie said. "Then we continue our mission and break our men out of the camp. Do I have that right?"

"That's the idea," McMahon told him.

"Good."

Braddock wondered if they'd ever get there. Behind the scenes, colossal forces were at work. Hundreds of ships, thousands of planes, millions of servicemen, and an endless supply of ordnance had ravaged Japan. This vast war machine was now aimed at the empire's jugular. Operation Downfall had begun, and it promised to be bloody.

Whatever the value of rescuing PWs, it wasn't the priority. The priority was crushing Japan's will to fight. Ending the war so all the PWs could come home.

In the end, Braddock agreed with Charlie. Whatever was going to happen at Hiroshima, it better be worth it.

Hiroshima, Japan, population 350,000.

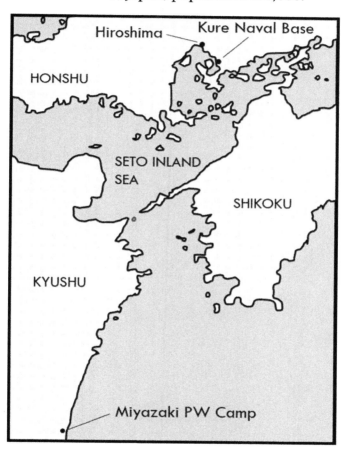

CHAPTER THIRTY-FOUR

HIROSHIMA

Captain McMahon scowled in the tense and crowded conning tower. This simple mission—surface, observe, report—would be one of the most dangerous his crew had ever attempted.

In just a few minutes, the *Swordfish* would surface in Hiroshima Bay exposed in the morning sun's full light. While the American Navy operated with virtual impunity off Japan's eastern coast, those ships had air cover.

Here, the *Swordfish* was a lone sub with its ass hanging in the wind, almost begging to be sunk by interceptors and coastal guns. Islands, all of them likely fortified against invasion, surrounded Hiroshima Bay.

"It's a little late in the game to be taking a big risk," the captain muttered to himself, though everybody heard it.

They were almost home. Nobody wanted to be the last casualty in the war. Standing near the

TDC, Braddock couldn't agree more. Surviving one sinking boat was enough to last him a lifetime.

The mission itself still made no sense to him. They were supposed to observe an attack. Heavy bombers had already burned more than sixty-five cities to the ground. What could they do to Hiroshima that they hadn't done to other cities in spades?

It promised to be spectacular, but promises meant nothing to Braddock.

And wasn't that just the Navy? You sign up to fix boat machines, and the next thing you know, you're on Saipan with hundreds of screaming Japanese chasing you with bayonets. You put together a mission to rescue Americans languishing in prison, and next thing, you're cruising in broad daylight off the coast of a country that uses suicide pilots to attack ships.

Thirty minutes, from 0800 to 0830. That's what the Navy required, and that's what McMahon would give them. No more, no less.

At the plotting table, Harrison inspected their position. If he was scared, he didn't show it.

"Where are we now, sir?" Braddock asked him.

"Close. We're cruising between the islands of Itsukushima and Onasabi." Charlie checked the clock. "We'll be on station about ten minutes ahead of schedule."

The man was smiling. He seemed downright happy to be back at work.

"Up scope." Captain McMahon settled in behind the periscope, circling.

"What do you see, Captain?" Charlie said, no doubt missing the days when he stood behind the periscope and was the submarine's eyes.

"It's a beautiful day up there. Down scope."

"Do you mind if I join you topside for the observation?"

"Be my guest, Commander."

"Permission to go as well, Captain?" Braddock said.

"Why not? Just note if we're diving, we're doing it fast." The captain sighed, resigned to his duty. "All right then. Rig to surface, Exec."

"Aye, aye, Skipper." The executive officer keyed the 1MC and said, "All compartments, rig to surface." He hung up the 1MC. "Maneuvering, stand by to switch from motors to diesels. On surfacing, answer bells on all main engines."

The yeoman handed out pairs of black sunglasses to anybody going up.

"What's this for, Yeo?" Braddock said.

"Beats me, Chief," the kid said. "I just do what I'm told."

Still smiling, Charlie slipped his glasses into his breast pocket.

"What are you thinking, sir?" Braddock asked him.

"That we're in for some serious fireworks."

"You think it's some kind of super weapon?"

"I don't know," Charlie said. "Whatever it is, if it's powerful enough to convince the Japs to surrender, I'll be happy."

"Ready to surface in every respect, Captain," the exec reported.

"Very well." McMahon checked his watch. "It's showtime. Surface!"

"Control, blow all main ballast. Blow negative."

High-pressure air shot into the ballast tanks, pushing out the water and buoying the boat, which ascended under the planesmen's control.

"Deck gun crew, stand by," said the captain. "We'll shout if we need you."

The *Swordfish* broke the surface and settled on the water. The lookouts mounted to the bridge and called down the all clear. With binoculars slung around their necks, the captain and some of his petty officers went up next. All four engines roared to life, ready to give the boat full propulsion if she needed it.

Braddock pocketed his sunglasses and followed Charlie into the warm sunshine topside. There, he found the *Swordfish* cruising in a northwesterly direction just north of Onasabi Island and five miles from the port of Hiroshima.

For the first time, he saw the country he'd been fighting against for nearly four years.

Lush green hills rose from Hiroshima Bay's placid waters. Fishing boats crowded the extensive waterfront piers. The Ota River and its tributaries flowed through the city and emptied into the inland sea, separating sections of the city linked by bridges. Wood and paper houses, shops, and timber workshops, all with curiously curved tile roofs, crammed the available land space. A few pagodas and grand administrative buildings towered over the rest. Banging out war goods, big industrial plants ringed the city. Beyond, purple mountains lay stacked in rows along the northern horizon, under a clear blue sky.

Alien and beautiful, like something from a fairy tale.

On the cigarette deck, a sailor fiddled with a film camera, trying to mount it on a tripod. If they had to make an emergency dive, Braddock hoped the kid would be able to get down the ladder quickly enough.

"Bridge, Conn," the bridge speaker blared. "Pearl confirmed the package is en route from Tinian and will arrive on schedule."

"Very well." McMahon ranged with his binoculars. "If the Japs see us, they aren't doing anything about it yet."

"They see us." Charlie swept the city with his

own binoculars. "Probably saving their frying pans for bigger fish."

The captain grunted. "I'll count my blessings once we're out of these waters."

"Planes, far, approaching, bearing two-five-oh," a lookout cried.

McMahon wheeled. "Got 'em. Three B-29s. That's our boys." He glanced at the sailor behind the film camera. "Start rolling."

The heavy bombers had flown over Shikoku at 30,000 feet, too high for Japanese interceptors and AA fire.

The sailor said, "What am I shooting, sir?"

"The city."

"What part of the city?"

"I don't know. The city. Get as much of it in frame as you can."

"Aye, Captain."

Braddock peered at Hiroshima, which was bustling in its morning routines without any signs of alarm. "They must have picked up the planes on radar. Why don't we hear air raid sirens?"

"Three planes," Russo, the burly quartermaster, answered him. "They probably figure it's no threat."

"If what we've been told is true, these three planes are about to kill a lot of civilians. Nobody's in the bomb shelters."

"They were warned," said Russo.

"He's right," McMahon said. "Our planes dropped leaflets. We warned them to get out of the cities. We warned them to give up."

"That don't make it right," Braddock growled.

"What do you think we've been doing the last four years, Chief?" Russo shook his head. "It's all necessary evil. Just a matter of scale, that's all."

"The scale never involved killing kids," Braddock said.

"It includes their cities, where they build bombs. The Japs should have taken their kids to the countryside by now. If they didn't, well, that's on them."

Macabre math. On Saipan, Smokey blew himself up with a grenade and saved three men, who killed twenty men and blew up a gun, thereby saving hundreds. At Hiroshima, if a super weapon killed thousands of people, it might end the war faster, which would save hundreds of thousands of American soldiers who might otherwise die during a land invasion. None of it had to balance. The only important thing was it all added in your favor.

Braddock shut up. It was easy to judge, but he didn't see any alternative. The war had to end. Any means to that end was, as the quartermaster had put it neatly enough for a poem, a necessary evil.

"Here they come," Captain McMahon called

out. "Sunglasses on, binoculars away. We'll have plenty of time to argue philosophy later."

The world dimmed as Braddock put his on. "Crazy thought, sir. Are we safe here?"

"I guess we're about to find that out, Chief."

When he'd heard about the attack, Braddock had naturally thought the Navy was overblowing how big this new weapon was going to be. Now he wondered if they were all underestimating it.

Russo frowned. "You think too much."

"Only in the Navy could thinking be called overthinking," Braddock shot back.

"Shut your traps, the two of you," the captain said.

Charlie slid his hands around the bridge coaming and gripped. His body clenched with tension, Braddock did the same.

The planes flew over the city. Nothing happened. They waited.

The world exploded in a blinding white flash that seared Braddock's eyes.

Moments later, the loudest, most terrifying explosion he'd ever heard flattened his eardrums.

He ducked and cried out, half-blind, his ears filled with a rumbling earthquake. His heart hammered in terror. The fillings in his teeth tingled. The air tasted like lead. He tore the sunglasses off in panic and flung them to the

238

deck, mindlessly shouting every obscenity he knew into the roar.

The world returned, obscured by the explosion's after-image, a purple splotch.

The bomb had detonated at a height of about two thousand feet, transforming into a colossal fireball. The incredible downward force had vaporized a square mile and buckled the earth all the way to the waterfront, flattening buildings and kicking up a tidal wave of dust. A hot wind and swell raced from the shore to slam into the *Swordfish* with the force of a close-aboard depth charge.

"Jesus!" the kid behind the film camera screamed as the rushing wall of hot air struck them all. "Did you see that? Did you see it?"

The flaring bluish-white light turned yellow then orange against the scarred atmosphere. Enraged clouds of dust and smoke seethed as the shockwave pulsed. A great reddish-orange ball rose over the city now, its edges purplish gray like a festering wound, its heart glowing impossibly bright.

The smoldering cloud expanded as convection currents sucked tons of dirt into it. Flames raged outside the blast radius, quickly growing into a firestorm. More loud rumblings boomed as buildings crumbled. At the center of the disintegrating city, the cloud boiled and rose like a mushroom head, bright as a second sun over the Land of the Rising Sun, pulsing orange and red as fires raged and died at its roots.

The super weapon had destroyed Hiroshima as sure as the hand of God had obliterated Sodom. The explosion had vaporized the city center and left the rest ravaged by collapse and firestorms that surged up the sides of the nearby mountains. And above it all, the awful mushroom cloud boiled into the sky, rising on its plume 45,000 feet into the air and casting a dark pall over the once-thriving city that had become a graveyard.

Braddock gasped at the horror of it. He'd seen men die. He'd killed or helped kill plenty of them. He knew the bombing raids had razed huge swathes of Japan's great industrial centers. But this. This was a whole new ballgame, almost too much to fathom. A single bomb had wiped Hiroshima off the map. He'd seen the horrors of war, but humans just didn't do this to each other.

Until now.

Gray particles flurried across the bay. Tons of earth, buildings, and people destroyed and sucked up into the atmosphere, returning to the earth as ash.

Beside him, Charlie fell wide-eyed to his knees, still trying to process what he'd witnessed. This wasn't war anymore. It was brutal extermination.

240

Annihilation of an enemy no longer regarded as human. No longer a heroic duel of men and nations, a contest involving honor and destiny. This was death and destruction on an unfathomable scale. The bomb had robbed war of all its meaning, delivering victory as an end justifying any means necessary.

Together, Braddock and Charlie regarded the destruction of Hiroshima like pilgrims struck by a vision of an angry new god.

The bombing of Hiroshima by the *Enola Gay*, which dropped the Little Boy atom bomb at 0815 on August 6, 1945. The bomb fell for 44 seconds before exploding some 2,000 feet above the earth. Within 1–1.5 miles around ground zero, marked by the interior contoured line, nearly nine in ten people were killed in an instant, and the blast and firestorm destroyed all buildings. From 1–2.5 miles around ground zero, marked by the exterior contoured line, about one in four were killed instantly, four in ten were wounded, and buildings were partly destroyed. Outside the second contoured line was ground at higher elevation, which sustained little damage.

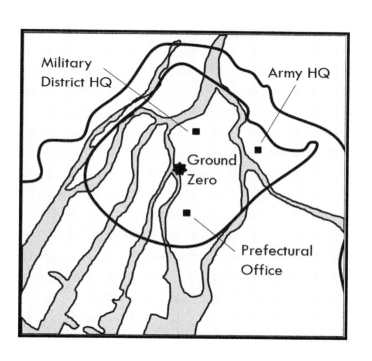

Military
District HQ

Army HQ

Ground
Zero

Prefectural
Office

CHARLIE

CHAPTER THIRTY-FIVE

ATOMIC WAR

Sitting in the wardroom with Captain McMahon, Charlie listened to a radio broadcast that was transmitted across the Pacific. His mug of coffee went cold as President Harry S. Truman described the awesome weapon that had obliterated Hiroshima. For the first time since his captivity, he'd lost his appetite.

The president called it the "atomic bomb," which harnessed the power of the sun. More explosive than 20,000 tons of TNT, it was 2,000 times more powerful than the British Grand Slam, previously the largest bomb ever used in war.

"It was to spare the Japanese people from utter destruction that the ultimatum of July 26 was issued at Potsdam," the president said. *"Their leaders promptly rejected that ultimatum. If they do not now accept our terms, they may expect a rain of ruin from the air, the like of which has never been seen on this earth."*

"This changes everything," McMahon said.

No response from the Japanese yet. Knowing Japan's stubborn military leaders, they wouldn't give up even now.

So the atomic bomb hadn't affected the Pacific War, at least not yet.

"Behind this air attack will follow sea and land forces in such numbers and power as they have not yet seen and with the fighting skill of which they are already well aware."

"It changes war itself," Charlie said.

If necessity was the mother of invention, its father was war. The Hiroshima bomb was just a baby, the prototype of even more destructive weapons to come. In the future, the great powers would build arsenals of these things. Charlie had heard the Germans had developed a fearsome ballistic missile called the "V2 rocket," a vengeance weapon that could deliver explosives from very long range. Combining the atomic bomb with rocketry gave rise to the possibility of submarines used as hidden, mobile platforms for firing atomic missiles at cities. A wolf pack loaded with such missiles could surface anywhere in the world and destroy a country in a day.

The atomic bomb would help America win her war against Japan, but future wars that used them would have no victors.

"We are now prepared to obliterate more rapidly and

completely every productive enterprise the Japanese have above ground in any city. We shall destroy their docks, their factories, and their communications. Let there be no mistake; we shall completely destroy Japan's power to make war."

Charlie said, "Any word from Pearl on the operation?"

Since the attack, the *Swordfish* had cruised south to resume its Inland Sea patrol, but was still no closer to raiding Miyazaki.

"They only said to hold station." McMahon jittered with excitement. "Big things are happening. The whole war is coming to a head."

"All the more reason to get our guys out. Once word about the attack gets around, the Japs at the camp will take it out on the prisoners."

"I get it. But orders are orders."

"We could be doing it right now. Pearl just has to make it the priority."

"We don't have the big picture."

Charlie vented his frustration with a sigh. "What am I doing here?"

He needed the kind of medical care the pharmacist's mate couldn't give him aboard a submarine. While his mind and soul benefited from being here, his body needed examination and treatment by doctors who had the resources to heal him.

Rest and proper nutrition had delivered partial

recovery from beriberi and scurvy over the past few weeks, but he remained tired all the time. The slightest exertion still winded him. His feet tingled, and shooting pains made sleep difficult.

The longer he delayed getting the care he needed, the greater the chance of relapse and further illness. He was okay with the risks because he wanted to be here, but it had to mean something. It had to have a purpose.

He recalled Rusty and Percy bowing to him at the water spigot and wondered if they were still alive.

"If it were up to me, we'd be down there right now," the captain told him. "I want those prisoners out as bad as you."

"I know it."

"The priority, however, is to win the war."

Charlie scowled. He'd begun to suspect the rescue operation was more about public affairs than actually saving prisoners.

Look at me, he thought. *I'm starting to think like Braddock.*

McMahon said, "Hey, here's an idea. Next target we run into, I'll put you behind the scope the way Morton worked with O'Kane. Give you some action to take your mind off the wait. What do you say?"

For weeks, Charlie had chafed at having

nothing to do. He'd taken comfort in being in a familiar environment, watching familiar routines, but had felt like a passenger. He'd grown used to it, though. In many ways, the *Swordfish* was foreign turf, and he'd begun thinking about Tiburon with a growing longing.

He'd done his duty for the war and had wanted to go on helping, but after witnessing Hiroshima's destruction, it was over for him. Seeing the mushroom cloud rage to its awful height, all he could think about was the old woman who'd been kind to him and given him food when he needed it.

The war required nothing more from him anyway. The bomb had rendered individual action almost meaningless.

"It'd be an honor," he said. "But I'm rusty. I'm of no use for anything right now. I just want to get my men home safe."

"It's just as well. We're only sinking sampans at this point. Even the Bathtub is drying up. We've got Japan good and blockaded now."

Whatever his suspicions, Charlie had to trust Admiral Lockwood would eventually give the go-ahead for the operation.

He couldn't go home without his crew. He wouldn't be able to live with himself if he didn't save them. This was his mission now. This was his war.

CHAPTER THIRTY-SIX

THE EMPEROR

Nine days later, Charlie, Braddock, and Cotten leaned against the bridge coaming while another Japanese city burned on the horizon. Matsuyama, about the size of Duluth.

On August 8, the Soviets had finally declared war against Japan and steamrolled into Manchuria, smashing the vaunted Kwantung Army. On August 9, the second atomic bomb destroyed Nagasaki. All the while, Japan suffered continued bombings and blockades, her far-flung armies across the Pacific starving and low on ammunition.

"Why don't they just give up?" Cotten wondered.

Given new orders, the *Swordfish* had ceased hostilities yesterday as peace talks progressed. Below decks, her crew stayed glued to the radio, which issued regular updates. The suspicion was that America and Japan might declare peace today, though that didn't help the hapless souls of Matsuyama, bombed two days before.

"I don't know if they can," Charlie said, remembering what he'd learned about the Japanese mentality from Lt. Tanaka. "If they even know how."

The Scout cupped his hands to light a Lucky Strike. The smoke swirled away on the sea wind. "They better learn quick. Or there won't be anything left soon."

"The Japs' leaders have been telling them for years, if we win, we'll take their women and force their men into slavery."

Braddock snorted. "They might be half right."

"They also believe the legend that a divine wind will destroy any foreign army that tries to invade Japan. It's where the word *kamikaze* comes from."

"If they believe that then they're even bigger chumps than we are," the chief said. "People need stories to get them through losing as much as winning."

Black smoke smeared the blue skies over Matsuyama. The misery Japan had inflicted on so many peoples had arrived at its own shores. The divine wind had come home. More karma. They'd lived by *bushido*, and they were dying by it.

"As long as it has a happy ending for our side, I'm fine with it," Cotten said.

"We sold ourselves on this story of the war that we'd be brave and fight and there'd be a big climactic finish," Braddock said. "Like a movie."

"The atom bomb ain't climatic enough for you, Johnny?"

"Look at you." Braddock next gave Charlie a once-over. "And you, sir. This story doesn't get a happy ending. Nobody lives happily ever after."

Charlie wondered at that. He remembered his officers pressing him on what he'd do after the war. All he could say at that point was he'd take some time. The war had demanded so much that at the time it had been hard to imagine anything past its end. It had been hard to imagine the war ending at all.

He'd signed up to find himself, and he had. Whatever his flaws, he'd discovered a capable man who tried his best and never backed down.

The war had exacted a hell of a price for this discovery, however. At twenty-seven, he was even more battered and scarred than the *Sandtiger* on her final patrol.

Happily ever after, he thought. Did Prince Charming scream in his sleep as he relived his fight against the dragon?

He said, "You don't think the war was worth fighting?"

"I saw the propaganda machine close up and personal. Propaganda that made those people out to be yellow monkeys needing wholesale extermination. If you have to swallow a big lie to fight a war, what does that tell you?"

"Okay, fine. Everything's just a big sham. Why did you fight then?"

"The Japs didn't give us a choice. The Navy didn't give me one neither."

"You joined the Navy thinking you'd never go to war?"

"I never said I was smart, sir," Braddock said. "I thought the isolationists would win out."

"The quartermaster was right about you." Cotten flicked his cigarette into the foam. "You think too much."

"Somebody has to. All I'm saying is, aside from getting us out of harm's way, winning don't mean all that much for men like us. Either way, we have to live with what they did to us and what we did to them."

Winning meant something to Charlie. Despite its cost, the war had brought America together and made her a great power, a source of pride. For him, it had bared his soul and taught him about life and death. It had been worth fighting.

He didn't voice these thoughts aloud because he knew Braddock would ruin it.

Cotten broke the silence. "I like my story better than yours."

"Don't worry," Braddock said. "You'll get more of it. We'll be fighting the Reds next. The only moral of the story is the more things change, the more they—"

An exultant clamor boiled up from the control room. From every corner of the ship, wild cheering built and spread. Soon, the lookouts and the officer of the deck were all cheering, while the three veterans brooded.

The war was over.

Charlie checked his watch. It was 1309. And today was V-J Day.

Everything had just changed, but Braddock was right, he didn't feel anything. Just tremendous weariness. A yawning emptiness no amount of fanfare could fill.

"I'll tell you one thing, though," Cotten said. "I'll never understand why I survived Saipan and my team bit the dust."

For each American who'd fought, the end of the story came with the search for meaning.

"You found your man, didn't you?" Braddock said. "Fought your way across Saipan to do it. Everybody gets a chance at redemption."

"But few earn it."

The chief shook his head. "In my book, trying is more than most men would do. It's enough."

Charlie gazed across the calm blue sea. How

had he survived, when so many times he would have been killed if he'd stepped right instead of left, looked up instead of down, run instead of walked? What would have happened if his torpedo hadn't circled back? Did hitting the *Yamato* or anything else he almost perished for really make a difference in the war? Why did Captain Kane die in the horrible midnight battle with the *Mizukaze*, while he'd survived? Why did Lt. Tanaka, who didn't believe the war was worth fighting, sacrifice his life to kill one man?

Would he ever forgive the Japanese? Would he ever be able to forget the worst of it all?

He could spend the rest of his life pondering such questions and never come up with satisfying answers.

In any case, his fight was over.

"We're going home, gents," Braddock said.

Captain McMahon mounted to the bridge. He shook hands with the officer on deck and each of the lookouts. Then he noticed the three veterans.

He said, "I guess you heard."

Charlie extended his hand. "We did."

They shook hands warmly.

McMahon held up a piece of paper. "From ComSubPac. 'The long-awaited day has come, and ceasefire has been sounded. As force commander, I desire to congratulate each and every officer and man of the Submarine Force upon a job superbly well done. My admiration for your daring skill, initiative, determination, and loyalty cannot be adequately expressed. Whether you fought in enemy waters or whether you sweated at bases or in tenders, you have all contributed to the end, which has this day been achieved.'" He paused, choking a little on the words. "'You have deserved the lasting peace, which we all hope has been won for future generations. May God rest the gallant souls of those missing, presumed lost.'"

"Well put," Braddock said.

Charlie agreed. He and his comrades in the boats had been lucky to have Lockwood as force commander. The admiral truly cared about his men. "What's next for us, Captain?"

McMahon grinned. "Now we go get your guys, Commander."

Charlie blew a sigh of relief. His heart lightened as four years of tension drained from him in an instant. His war wasn't over yet. He still had one last thing to do.

And even then, he knew, the story would go on.

His was a story that wasn't ending, but rather getting ready to carry on from a new beginning.

,

CHAPTER THIRTY-SEVEN
RETURN TO MIYAZAKI

The *Swordfish* cruised off the eastern coast of Kyushu. Captain McMahon scanned the shore. To the north, Miyazaki offered easy landing at its beaches, but McMahon didn't want to risk it.

The war was over. The emperor had ordered his subjects to lay down arms. Nonetheless, the captain wasn't taking chances.

The submarine rounded a point and approached a geographical feature McMahon identified as the Horikiri Pass. According to naval intelligence, the prison camp was a half-mile inland from there.

Charlie studied the rollers lapping the rocky coastline, grateful he didn't have to scale a plunging basalt cliff again as he had on Saipan.

"It still won't be easy," Cotten said. "Lines of rocks jut from the water about 200 feet from the coast. Beautiful to look at but deadly for rafts. We're going in nice and careful."

"Fine." Charlie didn't care because, for the first

time since the *Sandtiger,* he felt useful. For the first time since the brutal camp, he had something to fight.

And finally, he'd fulfill his duty to his men by bringing them home. His stomach flipped in anticipation and anxiety. He hoped he'd find them alive and in good health. Then he cursed himself for hoping.

Braddock mounted to the bridge carrying a BAR and bag bulging with ammo. "Just like old times, huh, sir?" He punned, "Once more onto the beach."

"Third time's a charm, Chief," Charlie said.

"Oh, I feel real lucky, sir."

"I know this is the part where I say I'm glad you're here and then you bitch I'm leading you to certain death, but I'll say it anyway. I'm glad to have you with me."

Braddock appraised him as if deciding how hard to slam him with a nice, juicy barb. Then he shrugged. "I'm actually glad to be here too."

Charlie smirked. "Now there's a first."

Cotten shook his head. "You two. Like an old married couple."

The submarine ascended until her main deck was awash, ideal for launching rafts toward shore. Bristling with weapons, the squad of eight Scouts and the *Swordfish*'s pharmacist's mate piled gear and supplies into theirs and started paddling. The sailors pumped carbon dioxide into another raft, which inflated with a loud *crack*. Three minutes later, Cotten and Braddock climbed in and helped Charlie, who hated that he still needed assistance to do basic submarining.

"Good luck to you men," McMahon called from the bridge. "Keep in radio contact. You run into trouble, we'll send help."

"Thank you, Captain," Charlie said.

"Godspeed, Commander. I hope you find your men safe and sound."

"Boys," the Scout said with a grin, "we're wearing the first American boots to step onto the Japanese home islands since the start of the war." He glanced at Charlie. "Not counting, uh, prisoners. You sure you don't want a gun?"

Charlie settled into the raft and adjusted his Mae West. "I'm sure."

He wasn't in any condition for hard combat. He hadn't said anything, but while his health was stable, he wasn't getting stronger. The only thing holding him together, he suspected, was his mission to rescue his friends from captivity. Raw will and determination.

In the end, he decided to trust that the emperor's subjects would obey his command to lay down their arms.

The rafts plowed the calm sea, making way toward the rocks.

"Now this feels like the end," Cotten said. "This feels real."

Charlie had to agree. In minutes, he'd return to Japan, this time as an agent of a conquering power.

They reached the rigid sandstone rocks, which lay in neat lines radiating from shore, a formation like a washboard or the scales of a dead dragon.

"We get out here," Cotten said while they were still in the water.

They piled out and carried the raft through the warm surf, which became shallower until they set foot on dry rock. Past the sandstone, a hill covered in wild grass sloped 200 feet in the air.

Over the hill, they'd find the camp about a half mile inland.

Charlie huffed toward the top, lagging behind the others.

Braddock turned. "You need a hand, sir?"

"I'm not an invalid." He rested with his hands on his knees. To hell with his pride. "Yeah, give me a hand."

The chief wrapped Charlie's arm over his shoulders and helped him climb.

The top of the hill suggested a paradise. Majestic phoenix palm trees, a riot of red poinsettia trees, a panoramic view of the Pacific. The *Swordfish*, *Tetra*, and *Barracuda* lay surfaced off shore, launching a wave of bright yellow rafts that would ferry the prisoners aboard. Determined to reach the end of his personal war, Charlie ignored it and pressed on.

Cotten paused to consult his map. "Horikiri Pass. This is the road."

They followed it until the shabby wood walls of Miyazaki Branch Camp came into view. Khaki-clad soldiers stirred in the guard towers. The prisoners had harvested most of the vegetables from the sprawling garden, which was now bare. The sight of this place filled Charlie with loathing. He wanted to burn it down.

"So what exactly is the plan here?" Braddock wondered.

"We won," Cotten told him. "They lost. We walk right up to the gate and knock. Anybody starts shooting, we kill them all."

The chief paled. "Great plan, Jonas."

The Scouts spread out, preparing to defend the party if necessary. Charlie, Cotten, and Braddock walked up the road to the gate, which opened in welcome.

Beyond its doors, Sergeant Sano frowned. "You."

"I'm back, pilgrim," Charlie said.

"I am surprised."

"What are your orders?"

The sergeant glanced at the Scouts fanned out on the road. He returned his attention to Charlie. "The war is over."

"Good. Where are the prisoners?"

"I ordered them confined to barracks when we saw you coming."

"We're releasing them. Now. Any problem with that?"

"I will take you to the commander."

Charlie opened his mouth to tell the interpreter in charge of discipline what he thought of that but reconsidered. Until several days ago, all these heavily armed men had been bitter enemies. The ceasefire had done nothing to quell the hatred built up over years of warfare. Observing proper form would ease tensions.

"Very well," he said.

They followed him to the headquarters. Colonel Murata stood behind his desk and bowed to the Americans. "Konnichiwa."

"Tell him why we're here, Sergeant," Charlie ordered.

Sano had a brief exchange with the commander, who gestured at the phone on his desk. Braddock watched everything with wide eyes. He'd never communicated with one of the people he'd fought for the past four years.

"The commander says he will have to talk to Tokyo for orders," Sano said.

"How long will that take?"

"The situation in Tokyo is difficult. He say you come back in several days."

"Okay."

"It's okay?"

"Okay." Charlie slugged the commander in the face.

Even in his weakened state, he summoned enough force to knock the colonel sprawling on the floor. The man looked up and wiped blood from his nose.

So much for proper form.

Charlie stood over him and said, "Sergeant, tell the commander he has new orders. We're taking our men back now."

Another exchange, which ended in the colonel saying, "*Hai*."

"*Yoku yattane, Taisa* Murata," Charlie said. "*Arigato*." *Good job, Colonel. Thank you.*

"Very diplomatic, sir," Braddock said. Cotten laughed.

Charlie said, "Wait until you see my next trick. Sergeant Sano, where is Nakano-*san*?"

"Gone. Went to Kure before it was hit and has not come back."

"Then maybe our planes saved us the trouble of hanging him."

They returned to the compound. About eighty Americans milled around. Skeletal figures blinking in disbelief their living hell was over. Some cried. The Scouts mingled among them, shaking hands and handing out cigarettes.

"Christ," Cotten said. "Now that I'm seeing this, I'm surprised you didn't kill that son of a bitch."

"There's only one son of a bitch I'm interested in killing right now."

Lance Corporal Chiba approached, bowing and grinning like the clown he was. "*Konnichiwa*, Johnston-*san*. Big surprise. American friend. Americans good friends."

"Sergeant Sano."

"Yes?"

"Instruct *Heicho* Chiba to lend me his *katana*."

Sano translated, and the corporal did as he was told, joining Charlie in admiring it.

Charlie nodded to Cotten, who kicked out the man's legs. The chubby guard cried out as he fell to his knees. The Scouts raised their weapons to cover the surprised guards.

"*Iie*," the man gasped as Charlie unsheathed the gleaming samurai sword. "*Onegai shimasu. Gomen-nasai!*"

"What's he saying?" Braddock said.

Cotten spat. "He's begging. He's saying he's sorry. He ain't sorry yet."

Charlie raised the sword over his head while the prisoners gazed at him with blazing eyes. Sano took a step back, seemingly unsure whether to order his guards to intervene or make a run for it while he could.

"Do it," one of the prisoners snarled.

Braddock raised his hands. "Sir. The war's over."

Charlie sheathed the sword in its scabbard. Something he'd keep. For all Chiba had stolen from him, he'd taken the corporal's manhood in return.

"Sergeant Sano, instruct *Heicho* Chiba that he has three minutes to leave the camp before an American kills him."

Sano relayed the message, and Lance Corporal Chiba scrambled to his feet. *"Arigato gozimasu."*

The man ran toward the gate without looking back.

"Iiko," Charlie called after him. *Good dog.*

The prisoners hooted and hurled insults at him until he was gone.

It wasn't Charlie's recognition of the man's humanity that saved him. Charlie didn't see the Japanese as subhuman the way these guards had once regarded him. Chiba, however, was a monster, plain and simple. He had it coming.

What stopped him was Hiroshima.

Holding the sword, Charlie realized he could

never kill again. For as long as he lived, he'd never take another man's life.

Braddock blew out the deep breath he'd been holding. "You did the right thing, sir."

"He'll get what's coming to him another day," Cotten said.

Other Americans would end up giving Chiba justice. Once the war crimes tribunals started, either the man would face decades of hard labor or swing from a rope for all he'd done.

Charlie's eyes roamed the prisoners, who looked back at him, some with surprised recognition. His gaze settled on a single ragged stick figure that was barely recognizable as a man.

He approached this man, came to attention, and saluted. "Lieutenant-Commander Reilly. Welcome back, sir."

The shattered submarine captain sobbed as he returned the salute. "Thank you." His voice came out a whispered croak after months of disuse.

"You're safe now, Captain. We've come to take you home."

Sailors arrived from the three boats, including another two pharmacist's mates and men carrying stretchers. The *Swordfish*'s executive officer was in charge of this phase of the operation, getting all these men to the shore.

"Let's go," Charlie said.

Apparently amused at how Charlie had taken over the mission, Cotten smiled. "What's next?"

"What's next is we go to the base camp and get Rusty and Percy."

And if they weren't alive, he might have to rethink his vow never to kill again in anger.

"You heard the man, Johnny," Cotten said. "Let's get cracking."

Liking this kind of work, the Scouts grinned like wolves at the new orders and fell in behind the three veterans as they returned to the road.

Charlie spotted the women, hauling water as they always did this time of day. At the sight of the *gaijin*, they shrank into the ditch and bowed.

He smiled at the old woman, whose eyes widened in recognition.

Charlie removed a pack of cigarettes from his breast pocket. "Jonas, you have any smokes?"

The Scout handed over a pack of Lucky Strikes. "All I got."

Charlie handed them to the old woman.

She bowed. *"Arigato."*

The cigarettes were highly valuable; she could trade them for whatever she needed.

In return, he bowed. *"Arigato gozimasu."* The extraordinary kindness she'd showed him had given him hope and more than that, faith.

"You're full of surprises, sir," Braddock said.

They continued toward the base camp. The gates opened as they approached.

An unarmed Japanese soldier marched out, leading two Americans.

Rusty and Percy.

Charlie limped ahead of the others as fast as he could to embrace his friends.

His war was finally over.

CHAPTER THIRTY-EIGHT

RUSTY

Jam-packed with riders, the *Swordfish* made way on all four mains toward Third Fleet and its hospital ships.

McMahon granted Charlie permission to go topside for space and air. He and Rusty sat on the deck with mugs of coffee, reveling in the sunshine on their necks and the bow wake's sea spray in their faces.

Neither man said anything for a while. There was too much to say, and talking required much more energy than they were prepared to give. Honshu rolled by, more lush green and rocky coastline backed by rows of purple storybook mountain ranges. The *Swordfish* passed the Kii Peninsula, where American light cruisers and destroyers had hurled six-inch shells at a naval seaplane base near Kushimoto.

Charlie told Rusty about the horrific time on the hell ship, his escape after it was torpedoed,

Morrison's death, rescue by the *Thornfish*, and transfer to the *Swordfish*, which was bound for Miyazaki for a rescue operation.

The firebombing of sixty-five cities. The destruction of the Japanese fleet at Kure. Hiroshima. Nagasaki.

"I once told you that your career would make one hell of a movie," Rusty said. "I take it back. It's too horrific for a family audience."

"The people back home don't want to know the reality about the war."

"You sound like Braddock. If they did know, it would have been a hell of a lot harder to fight and win it. Would you want Evie to know?"

"I guess not," Charlie admitted. As long as America didn't trick itself into fighting another one anytime soon, he didn't care what they believed.

"I wouldn't want Lucy to know either. It's bad enough she thinks I'm dead."

"No, she doesn't. I told the captain of the *Thornfish*. He radioed Pearl. She's waiting for you, Rusty."

Rusty gripped Charlie's shoulder. He flinched at the sudden contact, and his own reaction irritated him.

"Thank you," his friend said.

"You would have done the—"

"Shut up and let me say it," Rusty said. "You

don't know what I would have done. You saved us, and you almost died for it. Thank you. I mean it."

"I'm just glad to see you. If you and Percy had been lost, I don't know."

They'd taken Rusty, Percy, and the worst-off from the prison base camp. Planes dropped supplies and provisions, so the remaining prisoners would be all right until other Allied forces could rescue them.

"You found us," Rusty said. "I know Percy appreciates it too, even though he isn't talking much. The Japs didn't just break his body in interrogation."

"So what about you? What happened after I left for Manchuria?"

"The base camp was another sort of hell, but a far kinder one. More rations, we were allowed to talk, and the prisoners got fewer beatings. With over five hundred prisoners, the guards were less likely to single you out. Some of them were real bastards but none like the Ogre. That's what me and Percy called Chiba."

"The shoe fits," Charlie said. "I took his *katana*."

"So that's whose sword you had when you showed up. You should have used it on him."

"I almost did. Then I figured General MacArthur's lawyers would take care of him. He's looking at hard labor or the gallows."

"Well, too bad," Rusty said.

"I did punch Colonel Murata in the face, though."

His friend laughed. "It's the little things, brother."

Charlie laughed too for the first time in almost a year. "They do help."

"After Hiroshima, the guards looked really scared for the first time. All the Japs told us was the Americans had destroyed a city with a new super weapon. A guard who was kind to us told us to watch out. The emperor was going to give a speech. Either Japan was surrendering, or Hirohito was going to order the prisoners shot before banding together for a last stand."

The day arrived. Wearing their dress uniforms, the guards restricted the prisoners to barracks and prostrated themselves as the emperor delivered his message over a loudspeaker. A recording made in Tokyo. Major French, a flyer who was the senior officer among the prisoners, had instructed the men to arm themselves with anything they could find.

"Luckily," Rusty went on, "it was surrender. We couldn't believe it. That night, though, some of the guards got drunk and tried to storm the barracks. They were going to kill us all for glory. The other guards stopped them. It was a near thing, though. We dog piled in front of the door to stop them from getting in."

After that, the camp crumbled. Some of the guards, including the camp commander, abandoned their posts, leaving a skeleton crew of guards to run the place. The prisoners took over and worked with the Japanese to keep the camp running.

"Some of the guards were good men," Rusty said. "I'll testify on their behalf if I have to." He paused and watched the sea roll by. "Our bombers had hit Miyazaki pretty hard. More than a third of the city burned to the ground. I saw the damage myself. I'd gone out with crews to help salvage. The Japs built their houses close together and made them out of wood and paper. They went up like kindling after the incendiaries hit. We painted 'PW' on the roofs of the buildings so we didn't get creamed."

A squadron of fighters buzzed the camp at low altitude. They tipped their wings to tell the prisoners America had not forgotten them.

"Then the bombers came," Rusty said. "They dropped steel drums on us. The guys went wild chasing them. One crashed through a roof and almost killed Major French. Supplies and plenty of it. Food, cigs, antibiotics, you name it. I was starting to hope, Charlie. Then you showed up out of the blue."

"That's a hell of a story," Charlie said.

They talked the entire day. A warm and placid

dusk settled over the Pacific. As the light dimmed, Japan disintegrated into a dark mass, ethereal and unknowable. It was time to go below to get their supper. Charlie wanted to check on Lt. Commander Reilly, but he didn't move. He'd missed his friend and enjoyed talking to him. Right now, the world felt safe.

Rusty gripped his shoulder again. Charlie didn't flinch this time.

"We thought you were dead," he said.

"You should know by now I'm damned hard to kill."

His friend laughed. "You and me both, apparently. We did it, brother. We survived."

CHAPTER THIRTY-NINE

SURRENDER

On September 2, 1945, Charlie convalesced in a bunk aboard the *Benevolence*. The ship was one of three hospital ships in a vast armada that steamed into Tokyo Bay. Third Fleet, arriving to receive the Japanese surrender.

Many of the PWs aboard the 15,000-ton ship had gone topside to catch a glimpse of the battleship *Missouri*, where the surrender ceremony would take place. Charlie remained in his bunk, his restless mind torn between memories of the war and thoughts about what he'd do now that there was peace. These days, he slept most of the time, but it eluded him now. Irritable and restless, he lit a cigarette.

The 500-foot-long hospital ship was a marvel. Commissioned earlier in the year, it had a bed capacity for 800 patients, though right now, Charlie suspected it housed far more souls than that. The floating hospital carried seventeen medical officers, thirty nurses, and 240 corpsmen, who cared for the men in wards and medical facilities spanning seven decks, including a surgery and numerous clinics.

He still couldn't believe he was here. Bunks with clean sheets, reading lamps, and a five-channel radio system. Weary women in white uniforms hustling on their never-ending medical errands. Corpsmen pushing wheelchairs and library carts loaded with books. Doctors diagnosing and treating his broken and diseased body. Hours of physical therapy, including massage and time in a whirlpool.

None of it seemed real. He felt like an empty shell in this paradise, his spirit carved up and buried with the *Sandtiger*, left to torment in Miyazaki, and dragged through purgatory on the *Swordfish*. He wondered how much of him would actually return to America.

"Charlie?"

He blinked and focused on the beautiful nurse rushing toward him in a haze of blinding white light, like an angel of mercy.

"Oh, Charlie!"

She sat on the bed and wrapped her arms around him, sobbing.

"Jane."

"I heard about the *Sandtiger* on the radio. I thought you were dead."

Somehow, he'd known she'd turn up here. Jane never missed the action.

She studied his face. "Look at you." Her soft fingers probed a scar that ran down the side of his forehead into his cheek. "What did they do to you?"

He said, "I'm glad to see you're okay."

But of course, she would be. Her tireless efforts to help save the shattered bodies of American servicemen had earned her more karma than most.

"Okay?" she wondered. "The war's finally over. I guess I'll find out soon whether I'm okay or not."

"You will be," he said. "You're the strongest person I know. You remind me of a crewman I lost. You did good in a war that saw a lot of bad. Always remember that."

"What about you? Are you okay?"

"The doctors tell me I have a long, hard road ahead of me."

Now that he'd fulfilled his mission to bring Rusty and Percy home, his body had taken that as a sign it was okay to finally collapse.

"You'll recover," Jane said. "You're the strongest person I know too." She laid her hand on his chest. "But are you okay?"

Charlie had thought his war ended with the rescue of his crewmen, but he suspected he might have been wrong. He worried his war might never be over. He would fight it for the rest of his life unless he found a way finally to put it behind him.

She leaned closer to him. His mind flashed to a tent in Saipan where they'd made love while guns crashed in the jungle.

He worked up a weak smile. "I guess I'll have to find that out too."

"Find me when it's over," she said. "If you don't, I'll find you. We'll go somewhere. Paris, Cuba, I don't care. We don't have to run, Charlie. We can escape. Just walk right out. We could be okay, together."

The electric moments he'd spent with Jane during the war had been fleeting. In his mind, she represented the present. Live for today because tomorrow may never come. Could they have a tomorrow?

"Nurse Larson." A grizzled medical officer worked his way down the row of bunks, inspecting charts. "Come here."

Jane furtively kissed her fingertips and touched his face. "You think about it, Charlie."

After the doctor left the ward with Jane in tow, Charlie hauled his aching form out of bed. He pulled his bathrobe over his pajamas and tucked his feet into slippers. Then he plodded topside to see the surrender.

The sailors lined the gunwales in pajamas or skivvy shirts and dungarees and hats. Others sat and talked among boxes of gear. Charlie closed his eyes and tilted his head back to feel the sea breeze and the early morning's warm sunlight on his face. Waves of planes roared overhead to buzz Tokyo with a show of American military might.

Rusty sat cross-legged on a crate. "Over here, Charlie."

He limped over and lit a cigarette. "You always liked history. We're about to see it being made."

"Hell, brother, I've been living it for four years."

"Where's Percy?"

Rusty slouched. "He's got a difficult road ahead of him."

The wards were full of men with mental as well as physical wounds. At first, they couldn't believe they'd been rescued. They marveled at their new basic comforts. Then the malaise set in. Jubilation bled away to reveal shock, anxiety, despondence, and terror. They squirreled away bits of food in their mattress, screamed in their sleep, and shrank in panic at being touched. Percy kept referring to himself as a ghost. Charlie decided he would visit him again that afternoon.

"What about you? How are you doing?"

"I'm going home," his friend said. "I'm going home to Lucy and Rusty Junior. I'm going to love my wife and watch my son grow up. I'm going to have as big a family as I can. And brother, I pity the son of a bitch who tries to stop me."

Charlie smirked. "I pity him too."

"What about you?"

Home. Home sounded good right now. Tiburon. His mother and sisters. Evie.

Where he'd put the war behind him.

Jane would understand.

"Charlie?"

Before he could answer, a jubilant cheer swept the deck. Word was spreading that the Japanese had signed the instrument of surrender, and General MacArthur and representatives of the Allied powers had accepted it. History being made.

Charlie's mind was elsewhere.

Home. Yes. That was where he'd meet the man he'd become in peace.

CHAPTER FORTY

HOME

In the winter of 1945, Charlie arrived in San Francisco by steamer. He had no sooner crossed the gangplank when Evie threw herself at him.

He dropped his sea bag just in time to catch her in a whirling embrace. Her warm body melted into his, intoxicating him with her soft touch and floral scent.

Then she kissed him hard enough to make him forget everything.

The moment he saw her, he knew he'd made the right call.

"It's so good to see you," she breathed into his ear, making him tingle.

"It's good to be with you. It's good to be home."

"Everybody's waiting for you. Your mom's gonna flip."

Charlie couldn't wait to see his family and Tiburon again, but he also dreaded the prospect. Through his continuing recovery, the man he saw in the mirror every day was a shadow of what he'd been. It would break his mother's heart because she cared far more about his wellbeing than she did his service and medals.

"I don't know if I'm ready just yet," he said. "Let's take a walk first."

Evie broke the embrace and peered up at him. "You look good."

She'd always been able to read his mind. The tears welling in her eyes belied that statement, but he believed, scars and all, he still looked good to her.

"You're even more beautiful than I remember."

Evie slipped her arm under his. "We'll catch a later ferry then. Shall we go, darling?"

Charlie shouldered his sea bag. Together, they strolled away from the piers. Their aimless wandering took them to the fisherman's wharf district.

Evie's usual good humor evaporated into a dark cloud. "Things are calm now, but boy, you should have seen it when the war ended. On V-E Day, there was this eerie silence. Nobody could believe the Nazis quit. On V-J Day, the servicemen ran wild in the streets, drinking and rioting. They lost their minds for one long night. Some people got killed."

"That's terrible," Charlie said.

He asked a few questions about the riot, but she didn't answer. She just kept glowering. Finally, he couldn't stand it. "What's wrong? Did something happen?"

"Charlie, I need to get some things straight with you."

"Like what?"

She stopped walking and withdrew her arm from his.

Then she socked him in the shoulder. "Like that's for making me worry!"

She leaned bawling against his chest, and stunned, he held her.

"I'm sorry," he said.

"Tell me you're done with war."

"I'm done. I'm not even in the Navy anymore. ComSubPac gave me a medical discharge just before I left."

"And no more Navy words I don't understand," she wailed.

He smiled. "No more Navy words, I promise."

"Are you going to be okay?"

Charlie tightened his hug. "I'm going to be okay."

"Inside and out?"

"Inside and out, though I'll need your help."

"You know you got it. And what about us? Where do we stand, Charlie?"

"When you said you wanted to clear the air, you weren't kidding, were you?"

"Don't make me punch you again," she warned.

"If you'll have me, I'm going to marry you. Is that clear enough for you?"

She sobbed again, overcome with emotion. "Very clear."

"Is that a yes?"

Her crying turned to laughter. "Yes, it's a yes, you big dope."

He kissed the top of her head. "Anything else you want to know while we're clearing the air?"

"We'll need to invite John Braddock to the wedding."

Charlie reeled. "What?"

"John Braddock? He said he served with you."

"Yes, he was a chief on my boat. How do you know him?"

"He found me on the way back to the war after his war bonds tour," Evie said. "He told me you were alive and that he was trying to get you home. Was he the one who found you?"

Charlie shook his head in wonder. "As a matter of fact, he was."

"I made him promise he would. He kept it. You're lucky to have such a good friend."

Charlie stared at her for a while then burst out laughing.

She couldn't help but laugh with him. "What's so funny?"

That son of a bitch. The rescue had been his idea, not Lockwood's. The machinist had had the last laugh on him, a joke Charlie could laugh at too.

"Nothing," he said. "Nothing at all."

Evie nestled against him. "It's good to have you back, Charlie."

"I think I'm ready to go home."

Charlie and Evie caught the next ferry to Tiburon. To the next chapter in their lives, wherever their destiny would take them.

POSTSCRIPT

Charlie Harrison

Charlie married Evie Painter in January 1946. With his new wife and his mother, he traveled to the White House in Washington, DC, in March. There, standing alongside submarine ace Richard O'Kane and Marine flying ace Pappy Boyington, he received the Medal of Honor from President Truman for his actions during the Battle of Leyte Gulf. On the way back, he visited Chief McDonough's wife Florence and told her how Smokey saved his life aboard the *Sandtiger* and then gave his life to save his comrades on Saipan.

While he eventually recovered from his injuries, his nightmares lasted for many years, his scars a lifetime. As an employee for the Veterans Administration and volunteer for Veterans of Foreign Wars, he dedicated himself to helping veterans find work and adjust to civilian life.

He and Evie had three boys, Rusty, Lester,

and Charlie Junior. They in turn grew up to give Charlie and Evie seven grandchildren.

In 1947, he testified at the war crimes trials of Colonel Murata, Sergeant Sano, and Lance Corporal Chiba; Murata and Sano received life sentences, while Chiba was hanged in 1948. Otherwise, to his dying days, Charlie never talked about his experiences during the war, and true to his oath, he never fired a shot or struck a blow in anger again.

Having found and lost himself in adventure and combat during the war, he found himself again in peace and a home with Evie, though neither the war, nor the *Sandtiger* still on eternal patrol in the Philippine Sea, was ever far from his mind.

In 1999, suffering from dementia on his deathbed, he shouted his final words: "All ahead, emergency! Rig for collision!"

Gerald Percy

After his honorable discharge from the Navy, Percy boarded the first merchant marine that was leaving harbor and spent the next ten years wandering the globe. He returned to Eau Claire, Wisconsin, and took a job with Deere & Company selling tractors and machinery to farmers. He married and divorced three times.

In 1959, he achieved a major dream by being named *Bowling Magazine*'s Amateur Bowler of the Year.

Percy died of heart failure in 1981 while attending the Farm Tech Days convention and was survived by four children.

His funeral was the largest the city had ever seen.

Lester Morrison

On Charlie Harrison's recommendation, Morrison was posthumously awarded the Navy Cross for gallantry in his actions attempting to save the prisoners aboard the hell ship *Kyushu Maru* in July 1945.

Jonas Cotten

Cotten stayed in the Army for eight more years, serving in the Korean conflict. After leaving the service, he returned to Alabama but suffered from post-traumatic stress, alcoholism, and inability to adjust to civilian life.

In 1956, he moved to Alaska, stating he wanted to live as far from other human beings as possible. In 1959, he walked into the wilderness with his rifle and was never seen or heard from again.

Jane Larson

Jane stayed in Asia the rest of her life, working for various charities providing relief during the tumult of post-colonialism following WW2. In the 1960s, she helped shape the newly created Peace Corps and would continue her work as a field worker for five years before returning to private relief agencies. In 1968, she married a photographer but never had children.

In 1985, she wrote a book about her experiences abroad, which became a bestseller in the United States. In the book, she talks about her romance with a dashing young submarine officer during the war but doesn't mention Charlie by name. When Charlie read it, he was able to briefly remember the bright side of the war.

Jane died in 1994, mourned by all whose lives she touched, including Charlie.

John Braddock

Braddock returned to Detroit and accepted a job as a shop foreman at a General Motors plant, where he also served as a union steward in the United Automobile Workers. A misanthrope who loved humanity but despised most individuals, he worked tirelessly to ensure good working conditions for his men.

Always an agitator who hated war, in the late 1960s, he became an outspoken critic of the Vietnam War and married a peace activist twenty years his junior. They had two children together. In 1978, he was elected as a Democrat to the Michigan House of Representatives in District 9, representing Detroit and Dearborn. He retired in 1988 and passed away in 1995.

Russell Grady

Rusty returned to Pittsburgh and earned a doctorate in history thanks to the Servicemen's Readjustment Act, better known as the GI Bill, signed into law by Roosevelt months before his death. The GI Bill was a great success, improving employment prospects and average wages for veterans and eventually producing 14 Nobel laureates, three presidents, and three Supreme Court justices.

In 1952, he joined the RAND Corporation. From 1957–58, he consulted with California National Productions on *The Silent Service*, a television show dramatizing real submarine patrols during the war, including several episodes depicting Charlie's adventures on the S-55, *Sabertooth*, and *Sandtiger*.

He and Lucy had two more children, Mary and Charles. He kept in regular touch with Charlie until his captain passed away.

In 2018, Rusty turned 100. Many of his memories had become a fog, but he remembered plain as day Captain Harrison standing tall on the bridge, bellowing orders as he charged the *Yamato* off Samar.

And he thought, *Hang loose, brother. I'll see you topside soon.*

THE STORY OF CRASH DIVE

Thank you for reading the *Crash Dive* series! I hope you enjoyed reading about Charlie Harrison's adventures through the Pacific War as much as I did writing them. It was a real journey for me as a writer to explore this world, and I have to admit it's hard to say goodbye to it.

At its heart, *Crash Dive* is a series of short, simple, and pulpy adventure stories grounded in realism and authentic technical detail to make them come alive. Thematically, however, I aimed to go further than that, exploring numerous ideas related to war in general and World War II in particular, especially in the writing of *Over the Hill*. This was a war fought by the Greatest Generation, who were all too human. A war fought against an evil enemy, who often were only doing their own duty and saw themselves on the side of right. A "good" war fought for noble ideals, while being the most brutal and horrific in human history.

I owe a great debt to the submariners who

told their remarkable stories in numerous books, such as *War in the Boats*, *The War Below*, *The Silent Service in World War II*, *Clear the Bridge!*, *Thunder Below!*, *Submarine!*, among many other documents I researched to inspire and inform this series. *Crash Dive* is as much an homage to their service as it is a fresh retelling of historical events.

It is also the story of the submarines. When the war started, only about fifty submarines were in service; by the end of the war, some 180. Though hampered by faulty torpedoes, submarines sank more than 1,100 merchant ships with a tonnage of some 4.8 million by its end. They also sank about 200 warships, including eight carriers, a battleship, and eleven cruisers. Strangling Japan's economy and, by extension, its ability to fight made a major contribution to the American victory—a victory that seems inevitable today but was far from certain when the war began.

Japan's anti-submarine tactics and equipment were arguably poor compared to the war's other major combatants. Nonetheless, the Japanese sank more than fifty American submarines during the war, or about one in five boats. Nearly 3,500 submariners died in these actions—a casualty rate six times higher than the rest of the Navy—making submarine service far more dangerous than on a surface ship.

To all of you having served or now serving: Thank you for your service. And to all of my readers, thank you again for joining me on this voyage. Based on how well *Crash Dive* was received, I'm planning another historical military fiction series, which I hope to launch in 2019. Stay tuned for these and other new books at www.CraigDiLouie. com, and be sure to sign up for my mailing list here to stay up to date on new releases. I also welcome any correspondence about my fiction at Read@CraigDiLouie.com.

—Craig DiLouie
July 2018

ABOUT THE AUTHOR

Craig DiLouie is an author of popular thriller, apocalyptic/horror, and sci-fi/fantasy fiction.

In hundreds of reviews, Craig's novels have been praised for their strong characters, action, and gritty realism. Each book promises an exciting experience with people you'll care about in a world that feels real.

These works have been nominated for major literary awards such as the Bram Stoker Award and Audie Award, translated into multiple languages, and optioned for film. He is a member of the Horror Writers Association, International Thriller Writers, and Imaginative Fiction Writers Association.

Learn more at CraigDiLouie.com.

Printed in Great Britain
by Amazon